A Storm in Paradise

A novel by

Olympia Devine

Contents

Introduction: *A Storm in Paradise* deals with the fate of many individuals and the coincidences that brought lives together and tore them apart. Intrigue and conflict work hand in hand, stirring a storm of controversy.

The winds of change contribute to the life journey - a journey that reveals the fine line between love and hate, Godliness and lawlessness, generosity and greed, justice and injustice. In the end, one's self-worth and legacy must be examined without prejudice.

Influenced by true events, *A Storm in Paradise* contains the musing of its author; nonetheless, the controversies written reveal a series of coincidences that defy one's imagination.

a life's legacy

Chapter ONE

The glasslike turquoise sea of a tranquil Key Largo bay reflects a cloudless sunny morning. Tiki huts and a bar on the sandy white beach display some signs of life. The tranquility is shattered as a wave-runner bursts into view, zigzagging and spraying seawater to each side in deliberate showmanship.

Richard, a bear of a man, is the rider of the wave-runner. He is followed by another craft traveling a discreet distance behind him. Richard is in relatively good shape considering his 54 years. At 6 feet 2 inches, he looks too large for the machine and his orange life vest. From his carefree and confident attitude it is apparent he is adept at water sports and happiest in the lead. His golden hair is blown back from his slightly receding hairline and tanned face, and his hazel eyes narrow against the bright sun. He is trying to keep the engine from stalling by working the throttle, and his frustration is evident each time the engine slows down and splutters to a near stall.

He shouts back at the skinny, dark-haired wave-runner driver who has moved into position immediately behind him. He wants to be sure he is heard above the roar of his engine. His voice is tinged with sarcastic anger. “Hey, Kenny, did you do anything to this machine yesterday? Don't tell me I have to hire a mechanic. I already have you in the family!”

Visibly nervous, Kenny grimaces with a sheepish glare toward Richard's back, replying in a high-pitched voice, “These damn machines are just too old to keep working on, Richard - you need to replace them!” Kenny’s lean, bronzed body is drowning in an over-sized yellow life vest.

Richard's large, manicured hands shift and accelerate the throttle with confidence as he pulls farther away from Kenny. A thick gold chain hangs from one wrist and a gold Patek Philippe watch is strapped to the other.

Drowned out by his shrieking engine, Richard mutters angrily under his breath: “Spineless wimp! You know I tolerate you only for my wife's sake … if you weren’t her brother, I’d show you what my money will *not* do for you!” Leaving Kenny behind, Richard's attention is drawn to the beach area, which is still in view to the side. He turns sharply, spraying sea foam high into the air, and heads toward it.

In a zigzag, show-off pattern Richard passes close to the water's edge. His gaze focuses on a group of scantily clad girls near where his wife, Monika, is standing. Monika is watching him intently and is sipping from a glass held tightly in her hand. As he passes the group of girls, he makes eye contact with one of them who reciprocates with a coy, flirtatious smile. His machine idles as he slowly approaches Monika's position. She is short, small-boned, with shoulder-length blond hair. Almost childlike in her proportions, she is wearing a thong bikini and holds a hand above her eyes, squinting against the sun's glare. She could be any age, but her giveaway is her weathered 40-ish face bearing a mockery of a smile, as she watches Richard and Kenny with unmistakable annoyance.

As Richard's machine slows and drops lower into the water near her, she unexpectedly takes a few steps back, almost in retreat and panic. Richard is still out of earshot as she shakes her downcast head angrily, whispering to herself, “Can you believe it! Now he’s coming back here!”

Richard's wave-runner is spluttering while it slowly idles toward Monika. His expression softens as she looks up at him. His voice is warm-toned as he bellows above Kenny's engine behind him: “Hey, Babe! Want to hop on for a ride?”

Monika’s wide mouth curls in a half-sneer. Her lips have a hint of swelling from a recent collagen treatment and her voice has a shrill, accented edge as she snaps back. “I would rather stay at the bar and catch some rays. You carry on.” Her manner is much like that of a spoiled child who is sulking after not being able to get what she wants.

She turns briskly away after she has dismissed him. Her bikini thong exaggerates her small, tanned rear with its hint of cellulite. Her bleached blond hair shows no movement as she shakes her head. She has a fixed, spiteful look as she walks away with her head down.

Richard's reply is tossed at her retreating form. “Hey Babe, remember what you said - forgive and forget! This is supposed to be our reconciliation.” He grins as he directs the next comment at her rear: “Nice ass!” Then, throwing his head back with a laugh, he shrugs his shoulders and turns sharply.

Richard smiles broadly with a perfect capped-teeth grin as he once again passes the group of girls farther down the beach. He turns his wave-runner sharply, spraying a high seawater wake impressively from the side. He gets the expected reaction from the same young girl, who smiles at him coyly through strands of long blond hair. This time she leans into her hip, exposing an alluring hip bone, her fingers angled through the bikini tie.

Richard's wake just manages to unsteady Kenny, who is riding too close to him. Kenny is looking nervous. His lack of confidence shows as he pulls farther away from Richard's increasing frustration.

The ill feeling between the two men is evident and is replicated in the grimace of a third rider who now enters the scene. Richard acknowledges the new arrival with a brief wave and then quickly uses the same hand to twist the handlebar throttle to keep his wave-runner in motion. It’s clear the large, balding man is known to Richard as he waves back and circles around on his bigger craft, its engine’s deep roar evidence of its superior power. Circling, he comes closer to Richard whenever the latter's machine almost dies. Richard looks a little startled and yells above the mix of engine and wake noise, “Hey, Avi. Back off! You are getting a little too close. I can manage.” The balding man’s tanned upper torso is in perfect muscle tone and his dark eagle like eyes stare at Richard expectantly each time his engine splutters.

A dog is heard barking in the distance, and Avi yells at Richard in a heavily accented voice. “Okay, then, Richard. If you say you are all right, I’m going to pick up my dog. I left her on the beach. She likes to ride with me.” He turns his roaring craft sharply away, showing his prowess.

Richard and Kenny continue with a game of zigzag. Suddenly Richard's wave-runner sputters to a halt directly in front of Kenny's whose expression is frozen as he anticipates the inevitable collision. Almost before he should, Kenny leaps off his craft, plummeting into the mixture of seawater and spray. As his head bobs up out of the water, he begins to tread water. He shakes back his shoulder-length, black hair exposing his still frozen, fearful expression and watches silently as his driverless machine hits the side of Richard's with a sickening thud.

Richard is immediately catapulted, smoothly but harshly, into the water by the impact. He is underwater for only a moment before his large frame is lifted back to the surface by his life vest. His hair covers his eyes, obstructing his view. Visibly shaken, he quickly wipes the wet hair and salty water from his eyes. Treading water, he looks around to gauge his position and to find Kenny. He looks relieved to see Avi, who has returned and is leaning to one side on his wave-runner as his eyes cut back and forth, searching for the men. Avi spots Richard and starts circling him purposefully. The circle grows tighter and the sprayed wake adds to the confusion of man and water.

Richard can see Avi indistinctly through the spray now - he is heading at full throttle toward him and on a direct course to run him down. Richard waves frantically at him, but Avi seems intent on his course and may not be able to see Richard in the churning water.

Avi's powerful machine is only a few yards away from Richard's position when Richard realizes that it is not going to stop. He decides to take action and tries to dive out of the way. However, he finds that his life vest is buoyantly serving the wrong purpose now. His large hands struggle to free the front catches on his life vest. His frantic eyes show his panic as he screams at Avi, but the engine roar drowns out his futile attempt: "Avi! Avi! Hey! Stop! Damn it, can't you see me?"

Richard manages to get the last two catches of his vest undone, but the top one stays firmly intact. He takes a gulp of air and rolls into a partially submerged dive before Avi's hurtling machine is on top of him. A moment of relative quiet is left in Avi's foaming wake before Richard's head reappears. Richard's eyes are closed and his head tilts back, resting in the relief of the sun's rays on the water's surface.

Avi veers around and catches sight of Kenny who is staring at him, but remains motionless in the water a few yards away. Avi lifts a reassuring and triumphant arm as he calls out: "Can't see Richard. There is no-one else around. Good thing you have that yellow vest on. I am going to get help!" Avi speeds off at full throttle.

Kenny seems to have been waiting for this moment. He begins to swim directly toward Richard's orange life jacket. With his last stroke he reaches out to touch Richard's motionless head. He looks around one more time as he begins treading water and holding up Richard's bobbing head, which keeps slipping through the partly undone life vest. Eerily, Richard's machine continues to circle nearby.

There is no conversation between the two men in the water. Richard's large outstretched arms float limply just below the water's surface in submission to Kenny's weak hold and the elements. Kenny's head jerks from side to side, his frantic eyes searching the surface around him for any signs of life and Avi's return.

warriors of change…

Chapter TWO

Soft Natalie Cole notes drift through the warm, aroma-filled, candle-lit Palm Beach kitchen. A woman's elegant elbow rests on a green granite countertop; her long-fingered hand holds the phone's earpiece tightly between smooth blond tresses. Wet ocean-blue eyes stare at the cream-colored wall. The other hand holds a spilling champagne filled flute to her chest. Quivering lips are not sipping. A salty tear runs down her cheek to the corner of her wide, full-lipped mouth. Instinctively, her tongue tastes it and her eyes flicker as she tries to respond to the voice on the line. There is a moment of silence before the southern-accented voice on the other end of the phone line takes a deep breath, sucking air through teeth, making it obvious that this is an awkward task and unwanted conversation.

"Christina! Christina can you hear me? Did you hear what I just said? Richard is dead."

Christina finally finds her voice. She is ready to argue against this inevitable news. "He is only 54 years old! He can't be dead!" Her comment remains unanswered, and there is a brief silence, full of tears. "How am I going to tell Mark his father is dead?"

"I know…I tried to call you on your cell phone first and Mark answered. I didn't have the heart to tell him and thought it best you did it, anyway. I am really sorry. I know this is going to be a very difficult time for you both. And I'm sorry to be telling you only now. He died yesterday in Key Largo on a wave-runner, apparently of a heart attack. The crowd in Miami did not tell me until today. They were not going to tell you at all! I told them I couldn't believe that. After all, Mark is Richard's son."

Christina is beginning to deal with reality, and her reply is uttered through clenched teeth. "That is precisely why they would not want to tell us." She holds back sobs in a heaving chest as the words of the background music drifts through her soul. She is trying hard to focus on Anne's conversation, but the words of this song in some uncanny way seem to be meant specifically for her at this moment. "You and I could never be … with my very best I set you free … but most of all I wish you love." A slight smile forms at the corners of her mouth.

In her mixed South African and American accent she mumbles a barely audible response: “Thank you, Anne. I know this is hard for you. You are a precious friend and I’m grateful that it’s you telling me this. You have been one of the few who understood our crazy relationship and managed to stay friends with both of us.” After a difficult pause, she continues, “I really loved him, you know. Hell, I am so angry at him for being so damn stupid! I don’t know if I am angrier at him for marrying someone who was clearly only there for his money - or just mad at him for dying right now!” Her mood shifts and she stiffens her spine. She regains her composure and her characteristic stoicism.

The voice on the line is naturally raspy, but takes on a deeper, more concerned tone as it continues, “I know you loved him, and I know he loved you and Mark. He just never knew how to handle you. Do you want me to contact Richard’s office and find out when Monika and her Miami group are planning the funeral? I am sure they will not want any contact from you or Mark now. Not while they scramble through his financials.”

Christina’s back stiffens even more. Her attention is distracted by the sounds of a boiling pot. She shifts her athletic frame off the bar stool un-wrapping a long, bronzed leg from the stool's base. Her sandaled feet shuffle quickly across the marble floor tiles toward the forgotten pot of boiling water on the stove.

The waxy foam of boiling pasta is spilling over the sides of the pot. Simultaneously, a lean, dark-haired young man leaps into action from his frozen position at the kitchen table. She turns to look into his concerned brown eyes. She is surprised at her own complete lack of awareness. She has forgotten there was anyone else in the room. She steps back and allows him to rescue dinner.

"Yes, please, Anne, do that. I am sorry - I have a pot boiling on the stove. Good thing Lance is here. He just saved our dinner. Well, I have to tell Mark his father has died. He is with friends at dinner. This is going to be really tough on him. Thank heavens he saw Richard a week ago and they had a really good time together - at least he has that. He was so looking forward to a lunch they had planned this week. They were going to chat about his college choices."

"Are you sure you are okay Christina? I am pleased you are not alone right now. It is a pity I never got to meet Lance.

Ok, my friend, I will call you back as soon as I have news on the funeral arrangements. If you need anything, let me know."

The click of the phone line brings her back to the reality of the young man's stare. He is standing holding the spaghetti pot. A little lost in the moment, his eyes reflect her painful call. He asks, "What's happened?"

"Richard is dead. I need to find Mark and tell him," is her curt reply.

He places the pot on the granite kitchen top and turns with an outstretched hand to try comfort Christina. She shifts her position and moves away from him. Clearly, she is reluctant to let him in, while she absorbs the harsh news. She adopts a purposeful air and reaches for the keys on the table. He scoops them up before her fingers touch them. "I'll take you," he says. She nods, folds her arms across her chest and begins to shiver. Lance places an arm around her, blows out the candles and leads her to the door. She moves away from him with the excuse of finding a sweater and switching off the CD player.

Natalie Cole has the final words before Christina's impatient fingernail taps the CD button: "Smile, though your heart is breaking … that's the time you must keep on trying … you'll find that life is still worthwhile."

The evening air is heavy with the summer humidity. Lance is in the driver's seat of the SUV. The air conditioner and radio are on when Christina leaps in and reaches for her cell phone. She immediately opens her passenger window slightly and then just as quickly closes it, saying, "Sorry I just can't get out of some old South African habits. The air conditioner is obviously preferred."

Lance smiles at her. His eyes reflect confusion and personal hurt at being shut out of Christina's emotional moment, but he chooses not to address it. It is clear that Christina has changed, almost completely, in the instant of a phone call.

He listens intently as Christina's 'together' telephone voice asks Mark where he and his friends are dining. "Which restaurant?" she repeats. It is clear that Mark is pressing his mother for more information. "Mark, just wait there. Lance and I are on the way. Yes, I know where the Japanese restaurant is. No, I can't tell you on the phone! Just wait there. We will be there in ten minutes."

The trip continues in painful silence. Only the occasional squeeze of Christina's arm by Lance's young, strong hand acts as a distraction. He is trying, through his own confusion, to console her. She is staring ahead with a clear air of intent mixed with an obvious dread for what she is about to do.

As they pull up to the restaurant, a tall preppy young man walks up to Christina's side of the car. He bends down to her window, his intense hazel eyes fixed expectantly on her. He opens her car door with a large hand and says, "Okay, Mom, what is so important?"

She steps halfway out, one tanned leg framed by white shorts, not taking her eyes off his face. There is no hesitation. "Mark, your dad is dead. Apparently he had a heart attack yesterday on the wave-runner. I'm so sorry, son. You need to go tell your friends you are coming home with us."

Mark is silent. His face pales and his broad shoulders cave forward as he turns away, moving quickly back into the restaurant. He reappears just as fast and throws his large frame into the backseat. Both Lance and Christina look back at him and simultaneously say, "Are you okay?"

Mark is clearly shocked and does not immediately reply to the question. Instead, he wants to know more details about his father's death, which they explain they do not have yet. Then to their surprise Mark utters denial after denial. "I don't believe it. Oh, Mom, you know it is probably just a big hoax. Dad is just pretending to avoid some sort of IRS problem, or some other big litigation. He is always involved in something like that - larger than life itself!"

Christina's reply is gently firm. "Mark, I really believe your father is gone."

Mark's response reflects defiance. "We'll see. I will go to his office in the morning. We are going to have lunch this week. He promised." Christina and Lance look knowingly at each other.

Mark continues, "After all, we have to discuss my college. He said I need to make plans now. I have only six senior months left and he wants me to move to Miami. Dad promised me we would have lunch together, Mom…"

Christina turns and looks at her son's face. There is a faint glimmer of hope in his eyes, and she lowers the tone of her voice to almost a whisper. "Mark, I can't believe he is gone, either. He was not supposed to die, especially not now. He was so young. You know he is looking down on you right now and he will be there to guide you through the next few days…. and years ahead. You will need to be strong. I know you are. I do think you should go to the office tomorrow, but don't expect anyone to be sympathetic. I am sure Monika and her cronies are strategizing as we speak on how to keep you away. It may be too late already - they have had entirely too much time in his office since yesterday. You have to ask why they did not want you to know your father was dead, and were even trying to avoid telling you at all. I will contact your Uncle Andrew in Canada and see if he knows any more than this."

Mark does not reply but turns his gaze toward the window and looks blankly at the passing world. Christina stares straight ahead, deep in thought. Her exotic face is taut with a mixture of anger and grief. The car ride home is silent, and the heavy air is filled with mixed emotions.

At home, Mark leaves the car without a word and goes to his bedroom immediately. Lance indicates his compassion silently with a hand lifted toward Mark's departure, asking silently if they should follow. Christina shakes her head in reply, with the message that Mark should have his space.

Christina chooses to sit on one of the concrete lion statues at the patio entrance. Lance follows her lead and sits on the other. He gazes at her expectantly, as she rests her head against the green vines of the patio pillar. She shuts her eyes and sucks in a deep breath before offering Lance some needed matter-of-fact interaction. "He was not supposed to die. After all, who will I hate, or, as Mark says, love to hate the most now? We said so many goodbyes, but this one will be the toughest. You are not supposed to grieve for an ex-husband, are you? But he was my son's father, and this bonds two people for life. You know about that. You have children, too."

"Yep. I have terrific kids and a really bitter ex-wife. So I suppose I do understand. Perhaps more than I did before. There was obviously a time when you loved each other." Lance's reply is tinged with relief to finally be an active participant.

Christina's eyes open suddenly and she turns her head to look at him: "I knew this might happen, you know. I've been dreading this day, especially after he decided to marry the evil stepmother." She gives a bitter laugh at the name they had used jokingly at first and now use all the time. "The stage was set and the new life plan was launched into action. I always said to him that one day he would meet his match. He was a brilliant man, but lived his life too close to that fine line. I thank God I could raise my son at a bit of a distance from him. It was tough trying to provide a normal life for Mark. Balancing good life values and Richard's role in his life was not easy. Trying to protect him from the jet-setting superficial entourage as well as the money-hungry new wife has been awful! But then of course his dad would brag about the boats and private jets and pick him up from school in his limousine, saying it would all be his one day..."

Lance interjects with, "It really is not easy being a single parent and balancing both sides."

Christina nods her agreement. "I was pleased that Mark developed a good relationship with his father, especially in the last few years, and he is really proud of his father. Mark had finally reached the stage where they could relate to each other, and now he is gone. It's rather weird that both my father as well as Richard's died when we were seventeen, and now the exact same thing has happened to Mark. All heart attacks! It changes your whole direction in life, you know. I was headed to medical school and instead had to opt for the only thing I knew how to do - modeling. Funny how a hobby that my mother insisted I take up to help correct my awkward teenage years actually turned into my career. I will have to ensure Mark fulfills his college years. He is excited about it. He really wants to be a doctor."

Lance is looking positively relieved with the talkative Christina and replies, trying not to sound too enthusiastic, "Oh, I'm sure Richard provided for Mark's schooling. Mark did say they were chatting about it. So, he wants to be a doctor?"

"Yes, and it really is with no coaxing from me." She gives a half-laugh before continuing, "Although my mother, his grandmother, did drum it into him when he was little. Yes, I have no doubt Richard left Mark provided for. But I can't help having this strange feeling that this is just the beginning of a very long and difficult road for Mark. I know I am only going to be able to protect him up to a point. This Miami crowd is ruthless and they have shown Mark a very spiteful and greedy side every time he visited his father. Mark has handled it all so well, but he tends to internalize. I have been so proud of him. No matter what they did or said to him or his father, they remained father and son. Richard had a bad habit of allowing his staff and friends to fill his social circle and even influence his family decisions. He had an open-door policy, which gave them all a sense of entitlement. The smart ones knew exactly how to manipulate the manipulator. I am praying there are some kind souls among them now so Mark will be treated with the respect and dignity he deserves as Richard's son."

Lance stands up as he says, "How could they not? Mark is a really good kid and from the photos you showed me, he is the spitting image of Richard. It seems like he was the only solid tie between the two of you."

Christina nods to herself, continuing, "You are right. Richard really knew how to piss me off and I reacted as expected each time, resulting in twenty-five years of drama with countless international reconciliations - London, Paris, Cannes, Rome and more. Four bitter child-support litigations thrown in. I was the yo-yo and he was the string. The only true, believable witness to seventeen years of our life story was Mark. He really tried so hard not to take sides and to love us both. Thank heavens they spoke on Father's Day and I did overhear the 'I love you too, Dad.' They also had lunch in Miami a few days ago. I think I mentioned that to you?"

"Vaguely" Lance replies, encouraging her chatter.

"I was not going to go into the Miami restaurant after their lunch. I was going to wait for Mark in the car, but he called me on my cell and said his dad wanted to speak with me. That was really tough. I went inside for Mark. It was a little awkward in the beginning, especially when Richard complained that he was having a hard time with Monika and his stepchildren. He felt they didn't appreciate anything he did for them."

She laughs as she continues, "Richard said that his mother used to call Monika 'Christina' when she was in the hospital, pretending she was having one of her senile moments. Monika refused to visit her again. I really loved my mother-in-law. I have never met Monika, you know. Just could not meet the little witch! Everything was so clear from all that was said and reported back by friends. How the hell he managed to find another South African in Miami, God knows! All three wives, all of us, were born South African. This one is apparently close to my age, but a tiny spitfire! I was really shocked at the restaurant when Richard thanked me for raising such a fine young man, but of course he waited till Mark went to the washroom. I made him repeat it when Mark returned to the table. That was really nice. At least Mark has that!"

Lance gets up, saying, "Well, I'd better pick up my kids. Should I still bring them here for the night?" His look is hopeful but Christina reacts with a quick reply. "Rather not. It will be difficult on everyone - especially them. If you don't mind, I really should be here for Mark. Can we do dinner tomorrow?"

"No problem." He looks disappointed as he leans forward for a kiss goodbye and she turns her face quickly, reciprocating with a cheek, her right hand simultaneously reaching for the front door handle. He glances back at her as she quickly moves into the house. Closing the door, she rests her back against it. As though finally allowed to drop her guard, she sinks down as the flood of mascara-stained tears stream down her face onto the front of her pink sweater. She crumples silently to the floor, arms wrapped around bare knees. She rocks a little, back and forth, comforting her grief.

The sound of the phone breaks the home's silence and Christina stands up, wiping her face with the back of her sleeve. She looks up to see Mark in the doorway of his room. He looks down the stairs at her and she smiles up comfortingly at his hurt face. He smiles back. It is evident they have a strong connection. Words are unnecessary; they know each other well. Mark walks toward the sound and picks up the phone upstairs in Christina's bedroom. She stays motionless, almost reluctant to hear any further news. She listens for Mark's voice.

Mark is not showing any signs of grieving in his voice as he practices his excellent manners. He answers the caller's question, "Lance? Oh, he just left. Yes, Mom was supposed to have dinner with him tonight. Oh, yes, I like him. He makes her happy, but I don't believe she will spend the rest of her life with him. Hold on Jeanne. We just had some bad news, so she may want to call you back. I will let her tell you. Hold on a second."

Mark looks down at his mother. He whispers the caller's name to her. She shakes her head in response. Mark nods and continues his conversation with the caller, "Can Mom call you back tomorrow? Thanks!"

Christina climbs the stairs. Mark is waiting at the top and they hug each other briefly. She asks him again, "Are you sure you're okay?" He answers impatiently, "I am fine, Mom. I will deal with it all at the office in the morning."

Christina quickly changes the subject with, "Yes, your prediction about my future relationship with Lance is probably spot-on. Whatever connection I had with him before Anne's call was lost the instant she told me your father died."

In an attempt to comfort his mother and reassure himself, Mark responds with, "Mom, you and Dad must have loved each other a great deal to hate each other that much. Remember, I was in the middle of those crazy fights. You are both type-A personalities. It will be okay… you'll see. I just don't believe he is really dead. He might even be at the Seychelles island house. Or, keeping his head down because of his position as the Canadian Consul General for Liberia; remember the country is still in a civil war."

Two year old Mark's face is peeking from the top of the knapsack on Christina's back. His long chubby legs and sandaled feet are dangling from the holes cut in to the bag's base. He squeals with delight occasionally when Christina jumps over a rain puddle. The air is fresh from the recent storm and the glistening droplets on the large forest leaves reflect the new sunshine.

Christina looks back at Mark's face and points to the rainbow formed at the top of the hill. Mark's eyes shine with delight at the colorful sight. There is a tender moment of nature's awe between mother and son.

Christina has her camera in-hand and photographs the rainbow, then just as quickly the orange butterfly resting on the exotic yellow flower next to their path. Mark is twisting past his mother's shoulder to see all that the camera sees of this tropical wonderland... the Islands of the Seychelles.

The first trip to the Seychelles was with a group from Richard's office. It quickly became Christina's most favorite place to visit. The holiday home Richard shared with some of his business partners was built on the concept of a treehouse. Although the house foundations were firmly in the ground, it was built around a large tree with three floor levels. The open-plan island home was airy and surrounded by mountainous forests. The top of the walls did not touch the roof to allow for the free-flow of air, but this also allowed for rats and spiders - Christina's biggest fear at night, a situation which never failed to amuse Richard who would tease her relentlessly. The only road to the house was narrow and could only fit a small golf-cart size of car. Some of their happiest times were spent in this house with Mark allowed to roam free as a child - without fear.

In later years, this became Christina's refuge whenever there was another marriage reconciliation to their numerous separations. She would ask to go via the Seychelles to Canada or Florida. A route that was truly ridiculous since this is an island on the East Coast of Africa and Richard would agree - but let her know just how crazy it was.

Her visits had to stop after a reported failed government coup by a few South African ex mercenaries - who allegedly approached Richard for the money. No-one knew what happened to the house, but Richard was told the government had given it to the housekeeper. Christina was happy to know this and felt it was justly earned by the single parent housekeeper for the fifteen years she had taken care of the house - while the owners only visited a few times a year.

a bitter struggle fought…

Chapter THREE

"What do you mean there was a private viewing in Miami? If anyone was supposed to be there it should have been Mark. Damn it, Andrew. How can she be so vicious? Where is Richard's body now?" Christina's voice is tinged with controlled anger. She has her cell phone in hand. She is standing outside her large Palm Beach home. There are dark gray clouds looming in the distance. The sun is shining brightly on the two-storey house. It is a pink cookie-cutter style with lion statues at the entrance providing a touch of individuality. Dressed in a coral skirt-suit, she is standing in the driveway next to the SUV. Her business portfolio and keys are in hand shielding her face from the sun. The other hand has her cell phone pressed tightly to her ear.

"I thought you knew, Christina. Ah, hell, it was rough to see my brother lying there. You know, she had him dressed in cheesecloth. She didn't even put him in a suit! He was always such a snappy dresser. He deserved so much more. His was truly a rags-to-riches story. I selected a handsome copper urn with angels and she changed it to a cheaper plastic one! When I didn't see you there I thought you perhaps didn't want to be there. You mean no one from the office called Mark? Hell, I don't know where his body would be right now."

The caller, Richard's brother, Andrew, is distraught. "Even though I am acting as the estate's personal representative, I have no role in the funeral arrangements. Apparently it is the wife's prerogative - not me as his brother and estate personal representative. Monika has not been helpful since I got in from Canada. In fact she has been quite hostile. What are you going to do, Christina?"

Christina's knuckles are white as she clutches the phone to her ear. "Mark *will* see his father today. He must see him. He still thinks Richard is hiding out and will appear miraculously one day in his life. I'll call one of the idiots at Richard's office and head down to Miami in a few minutes. I'll call you back and let you know what happens."

"Okay, good luck!" is Andrew's reply, and Christina launches into a barrage of phone calls while walking back into the house, yelling for Mark.

"Mark! Mark! That damn bitch! She will rot in hell! She will not stop you from seeing your father. Come on, get dressed. We are going to Miami."

"What's going on, Mom?" Mark looks shocked as he peers down from the stair banister at his mother, who is raging and multi-tasking. She is making calls while closing downstairs windows as the ominous gray sky heralds another late afternoon Florida thunderstorm.

"Can you believe them? There was a viewing and they didn't even tell you. They have no respect for your father or you! We are going to see him, whether she likes it or not!"

Mark's face is pale as he says, "You mean he IS dead and we are going to see him?"

Christina stops at a window and notices a few raindrops hitting the glass. "Hurry, this storm is coming in fast. We may just manage to beat it!" She walks toward Mark who is now at the bottom of the stairs. He is dressed in jeans and a neat button-down shirt. His 6-foot-4-inch frame towers over his mother as she goes up to him. "I have never seen a dead body before, least of all someone I really loved! This is going to be extremely tough for both of us, but it has got to be done. Hopefully we can still see him before they send him to the crematorium." Mark's eyes show a slight hopeful glint. "Yeah, a hoax. There probably is no body at all. What happened to the meeting you were on your way to?"

Christina's eyes are focused. The corners of her mouth show a weary grimace as she turns to him and says, "Meeting canceled. I need to be with you and you need to be strong whatever happens in the next few hours." Mark follows his mother to the SUV as they run through the rain.

Christina's fingers are working the cell phone buttons faster than Mark has seen them move before and he is looking at her in amazement. He is driving and listening to her telephone conversations intently. The storm is noisy and she has to yell into the phone.

"James, you make damn sure Monika agrees. What do you mean; she has to give her permission for Mark to see his father? You call her right now and tell her we are on our way. She can't hurt Mark more than she already has. She has no idea who she is dealing with! What did you say? He's been moved to the crematorium? Why? Tell the funeral home to bring him back! We'll be there in an hour. This storm will not slow us down. If she doesn't agree, I will pay her a visit while I am down there. Oh, and yes I forgot to say thank you for taking Mark for lunch after she ordered him out of Richard's office. I know she thought he was there for a possible take-over bid. In reality he just needed to be close to his father's memory, and hopefully get more information on his death from the staff. Of course no-one was talking!"

The drive is filled with telephone calls and back-and-forth yelling. Christina glances at Mark's expression and realizes it has started to change from disbelief to one of sadness. "Its okay, Mark, we will make it and we will see this through. She will not get away with anything! She is in for the battle of her life. She thinks she is smarter than anyone else. You know she is probably searching through all your father's financial documents right now - trying to grab as much as she can before we do anything. She only ordered you out of your father's office on Monday to keep you out of the way – and away from your inheritance."

“It was a good thing I went to the office, Mom. I sat in Dad’s chair and at his desk for a while. It was weird, but I could still smell his cologne. I did notice that a few of his things are missing already. Like the silver-inlaid carved saddle he was so proud of.”

“I’m not surprised!” she replies and launches into another tirade without taking a breath. “Now we know why James paid us a visit yesterday. I am still trying to figure out why he kept trying to assure us your father died of a heart attack. Did you see how he kept looking around the house, trying to evaluate our financial strength? Probably thinking we may start litigation. There *should* be no reason to. The will and your father’s intentions for you were always very clear. I am pleased that, when James tried to bring it up, I told him I did not want to discuss the will until Richard was buried. Did you notice he had to agree when I asked him if he felt your father loved you and would always have taken care of you? Let’s see if he has helped us this time by calling Monika. Damn her! We have to ask her permission to view Richard’s body! James knew about this viewing yesterday and said nothing! Interestingly, your Uncle

Andrew told me that a twenty-two page pre-nup has surfaced. Your father only left her a motor car and a one-million-dollar life insurance policy."

Mark motions at the street sign as he looks at the scribbled directions in his mother's hands. He seems quite used to his mother's angry side, as he says, "More than she deserved. They were married for less than a year. I remember that pre-nup ordeal. Dad told her about the pre-nup just before the wedding date. She went nuts! He was going to call it all off, but then she signed and sulked for months. She still got her way with the marriage. It is strange that from the beginning she believed she would outlive Dad. Michael told me that she walked around for days telling people that Dad had left her absolutely nothing in the pre-nup."

Christina points out a sign on the right and they turn into the driveway. Christina remarks, "Looks closed … and fittingly drab. What happened to Michael by the way?"

Mark replies as they both get out of the car. "Nobody is quite sure. After Dad had the litigation with him he disappeared. It was inevitable that he would. He was truly hurt by it all. They were really close friends and loyal business partners. Monika definitely instigated that situation to gain full control. She worked on Dad's paranoia. She kept telling him she believed his friends were stealing from him – even accusing Michael!"

Christina shakes her head. Her response is almost a whisper as they enter through the open front door into a dark hallway. "Well, I suppose the open door means they might be expecting us. What nonsense, Michael was always his most loyal friend. He was with him for many years. I think I told you that and was even my driver before you were born. He did really well for himself to eventually become your Dad's partner…your Dad had to trust him for that to happen."

The narrow, dimly-lit hallway is very quiet. Mother and son stand motionless for a few seconds not sure where to go. A lean, dark-suited young man suddenly appears through a doorway startling mother and son. He looks just as surprised to see them. After introducing themselves, they ask him where they can view Richard. They are met with, "Sorry, ma'am, we had no idea you were coming and we are about to close. Mr. Richard St. John has already been moved to the crematorium across town. His wife gave us strict instructions to get this done as soon as possible. I was switching off the lights. I am the parlor aide."

The apologetic young man looks even more surprised as Christina takes his sleeve and leads him away from Mark to the adjacent hallway. She looks back at Mark and motions for him to wait there. He nods.

Christina's face is close to that of the pale, skinny young man. Her voice is a near whisper. Her face has a sense of urgency and the squeeze applied to the young man's arm proves her determination. "My son needs to see his father. He does not believe his father is dead. The new wife is trying to stop him from seeing him. I need you to call her and tell her we are here. We are not leaving until he is brought back. I am sorry if this is going to make for a late closing, but I really expect and need your help."

"Yes ma'am." Christina lets his arm go and he hurries away. It seems seconds before he returns and tells her that Richard is being brought back through the rush-hour traffic.

Christina and Mark thank him as they are seated in plush, gray-winged armchairs in the waiting room. The walls are lined with gray drapes. There is an open Bible to one side and a sign-in guest book on a wooden pedestal. Christina has her head back with eyes closed. Mother and son remain expectantly silent for the next half-hour, except for Mark's occasional fidgeting.

The storm seems to have followed them as the thunder breaks and they begin a whispered conversation in the dimly lit room. Christina looks at her son with deep concern as she comments, "You know what I think? Perhaps this is meant to be. Maybe Richard knows we both needed to have some quiet time with him, without his Miami entourage." Mark nods, saying, "Yes, that would have been very difficult."

The young man startles them as he enters their area and quietly motions them to another closed door, which he opens, ushering them into another very dimly lit room. The walls have warm wood and yellow accents. There is a large and elegant arrangement of white lilies to one side that Christina focuses on, trying not to look at the large wooden casket at the side of the room. It has been positioned at the appropriate viewing level. Mark is also trying to avoid the inevitable. He is looking at his mother, his head turned away from the casket.

The young man bows respectfully as he leaves them, closing the door behind him. Mother and son look startled as the door shuts. They stand motionless for a few moments, not sure what to do. Then they both turn to face the half-open casket.

Richard's face is tanned from his day on the wave-runner and there seems to be a slight smile at the corner of his mouth. His head is resting on a perfectly placed white pillow. The receding hairline frames a peaceful, unlined face, the dark blond hair combed back perfectly. His large, manicured hands are tied in a clasped position over his abnormally swollen chest. The cheesecloth is wrapped around him mummy-style with the casket open to his waist.

Christina is motionless, standing a distance away from the casket, Mark has moved next to his father. He has a look of disbelief as he says, “It looks like he is sleeping, Mom.”

Christina’s voice is strained but comforting. “Yes. He looks like he just got off the wave-runner a short while ago and now is resting. He looks good, even still has a tanned face. I am pleased you have this time with him. It’s a tough thing to do, but you would never have been sure he was dead.”

Then in a faint whisper she adds, “I can’t help feeling that there is a part of me in that casket.”

“Hey, at least he was enjoying what he liked to do best. He really loved being out on the water.”

They both smile. Christina looks at Mark saying, “I am sure your father is standing right here with you, Mark.”

Mark glances at her and says, “I know, Mom. I just can't believe Monika didn’t at least have him in a suit, one of his London-tailored suits. I heard you say she’d ordered a cheaper plastic urn to replace the copper one Uncle Andrew chose. No love lost there. It should be clear now what her real intentions were and are. She only married Dad for his money. Why didn't she at least give him the respect he deserved in death?”

Mark is touching his father’s hand. Christina answers his question with, “At least your Uncle Andrew tried. He said Monika had left strict instructions at the funeral home that no one was allowed to interfere with her funeral arrangements.”

Mark’s next shocked words are a complete interruption of the emotional moment, opening up a whole new dynamic to their presence in the room.

"Mom, Dad has no legs. Or, it might be one leg only!" Mark is peering down the gap under the casket lid at the simple cheesecloth covering him. Christina moves next to her son and both look through the casket gap. There has been an obvious attempt at scrunching the cheesecloth to form an appearance of legs. Mark's knees cave and he is now kneeling next to his father's casket. Christina offers a hollow explanation in an effort to relieve Mark's distress at seeing his larger-than-life father inexplicably mutilated.

"Don't be silly, Mark. Perhaps his legs just look smaller under the cloth." Mark is beginning to react to his father's death with rage.

Mark glares at her in disbelief. "Have a look. No! Mom, it's true. What did they do to him? Is this why they tried to stop me from seeing him? Why did they have their viewing this afternoon without me? Damn it, I am his son!"

Christina approaches the side of Richard's casket hesitantly and with a sense of total confusion, says, "Oh, my God! What happened to his legs? Who did this to him? The fact that his chest is so swollen may be because of the heart attack or drowning, but his legs? Before we leave we will ask them here if they know what happened."

The air in the room is heavy with emotion. Christina has a sense of urgency about her now as she says, "Mark, it is time to say goodbye. They will need to move him to the crematorium tonight." Both of them touch Richard's cheek. Their eyes are shuttered in a moment of communion with Richard's spirit.

"Mom, he feels so cold." Mark's face is perplexed at his observation. Christina reacts to his comment with a flood of tears. It is clear that both of them are finding it hard to leave.

One tear falls on Richard's cheek and mixes with the well-finished make-up. Mark brushes it away with the back of his hand before they leave Richard's side.

The parlor aide is standing a discreet distance away from the door as Mark opens it and squints at the brighter light. The young man immediately walks toward them, and Christina's impatience is evident as she asks, "Do you know what happened to his legs?" The young man looks startled, replying, "No, I am afraid not. You would have to ask his wife. We received the body in that condition."

There is no reply from mother and son to this statement. They exchange a knowing look and Christina's sarcastic glance is the only answer. They both shake the slender man's hand while thanking him for helping them so efficiently.

As they walk out into the hues of the Miami dusk, Mark looks at the sky and says, "The storm has blown over. It should be an easier drive back."

Sheba, the lion cub is being bottle fed and cradled by Mark's grandmother. The growling, teat-sucking cub can be mistaken for a large cat with her front paws holding onto the bottle together with that of her stand-in mother's hand. Six-year-old Mark is watching the process with great curiosity, hanging on his grandmother's every word. Christina is sitting next to them on the couch re-filling baby bottles.

" But Yaya, why does the milk for Sheba have to come from the same cow?"

Mark's grandmother, who is known affectionately as Yaya, looks up at him with a loving smile as she replies." Well, the cub would only be drinking milk from one mother and if we give her a different cow's milk she could get a tummy ache and then be very sick."

Mark's response is quick as he leans forward onto his folded arms on the couch armrest. "So, the cub knows she only has one real mother? But, I am sure she loves you too Yaya."

Yaya leans over to Mark and kisses him on his forehead as she replies. "Yes, this cub knows it was born to only one mother and Sheba will go back into the lion's area when she is strong and old enough. I am quite sure she will find her mother again - or her mother will find her. A mother and child love bond is very strong. She will also remember us as the family who raised her-because we loved each other too. "

Mark looks serious and says, "I also only have one mother, but I love you and Sheba too. You must not be sad when Sheba has to leave, we will always be together."

to change human thought…

Chapter FOUR

The large Miami event hall reflects funeral preparations. There is an obvious absence of religious emblems or décor, with sunlight streaming through windows onto the somber crowd-filled room. Some are seated, while others are drifting between the rows and chatting. Most are dressed in Miami black. Balding, suited men with ponytails are carrying briefcases as they take their seats. Bejeweled and augmented women are seated in the mix, some more tearful than others. There are distinctive young, single, attractive women arriving discreetly, taking their positions near the back of the hall. The observer is left wondering why there is no religious or a family introduction as the eulogies begin. The crowd becomes silently solemn as the ceremony unfolds.

Christina arrives just as the service begins. She has a friend with her, Jeanne Beaumont. As she enters, she is motioned to by a group of people already seated toward the back right. She nods her thanks and takes two seats close to them.

Christina glares at the podium as James begins his welcome speech to the crowd. He notices Christina's arrival and his expression betrays some strain. He introduces himself as Richard's good friend and proudly launches into impersonal, reminiscent banter about the "good party times" shared with Richard.

"We will miss him. He was a good friend. I will never forget the parties on the boat. Our hearts go out to his adoring wife, Monika, and her children, whom he adored; his brother, Andrew; his daughter, Samantha - and of course his son, Mark, whom he had just gotten to know."

On cue to the references made, Monika and her two sons who are seated in the front row proceed to cry and glance over their shoulders to see who is looking at them.

James begins to read Monika's strange poem dedicated to Richard. It is clearly an incoherent, spaced-out ramble that adds to the service's confusion. Many are left shaking their heads, mystified.

Christina nudges the older woman sitting next to her and whispers, "What nonsense! What a setup! Who the hell is James trying to convince? What a sad charade! Exactly what he wants everyone to believe about the only true heir to Richard's estate! What absolute nonsense! Hell, Jeanne, you know Mark has been close to his father most of his life and has not 'just got to know him!' The problem was me, not Mark! Poor Richard had to pretend he was not seeing his own son in the last few months. I am still not sure why he had to hide the fact and why he was so scared of Monika!"

The older woman replies with a knowing look, "From what I see here I would have been scared of this lot, too."

Christina cranes her neck looking for Mark's back, in the front rows, and whispers, "I wonder how Mark is doing."

Jeanne's reply is filled with sincerity. "After what he has been through in his life, I am sure he is the strongest person here. He is a true, gallant knight. I am very proud of him and the fact that I am his Catholic godmother."

James briefly mentions the fact that Richard was one of the most spiritual people he knew. He then repeats this fact looking around at the crowd, proudly believing he is making his eulogy connection, just as a robed priest approaches the podium.

Christina continues her angry whispering. She gestures with a finger toward James. "He had the audacity to come to our house three days after Richard died to try to convince us not to contest anything legally down the road. I know there is nothing to contest. I told him to wait at least until after Richard's funeral before discussing the finances. Silly fool! Can't believe that Richard's brother is not up there and why the hell they didn't invite him or Mark to speak."

Jeanne grimaces back at her, shaking her head. She then whispers a surprised statement in a low, raspy voice, "I didn't know he had a daughter." Christina also whispers her reply. "Nor did Richard! Or any of us! We only found out a few years ago. Apparently this is an illegitimate daughter from his earlier Canadian years who found him a couple of years ago."

Jeanne raises an eyebrow as both of them turn their attention to the well-spoken, middle-aged Catholic priest now at the podium. He delivers a sincere and moving eulogy for Richard's soul and ends it with the sad statement, "Although I did not know him, I am sure the number of people here today proves he left this world leaving many friends behind, so he must have made a difference in your lives. Let us say the Lord's Prayer. 'Our Father…'"

It is painfully clear that there are only a handful of mourners saying the prayer with the priest. Individual voices are heard clearly as an echo through the quiet, sullen air of the room. Christina and Jeanne are heard loud and clear above the silent rows in front of them. Some of who are glaring back at them in annoyance.

The service ends with a very moving musical selection by celebrity saxophone player Clarence Clemons. Christina turns to Jeanne with tear-filled eyes, whispering, "The priest and Clarence are probably the only parts that make this any type of normal funeral. Little doubt we have a few atheists or agnostics here today. You know, my first date with Richard was at a Johannesburg jazz club more than twenty-five years ago, and a saxophonist played. I'm not surprised he was friends with Clarence." She wipes the end of her nose with a soaked and crumpled tissue. Her eyes show the pain of her last statement. Then just as quickly she switches back to a mood of anger, continuing, "I can't believe there was no mention of Richard's amazing achievements. Not even the fact he was appointed the Canadian Consul General of Liberia. Richard was proud of how far he had come from his underprivileged roots."

Jeanne squeezes Christina's hand knowingly, and her voice is tinged with the wisdom of experience. "Perhaps this is all totally intentional, Christina. I think James's role right now is to convince everyone here that Mark was not an important part of Richard's life and so not part of his will or inheritance. Then in an effort to hide finances, he may even be trying to understate Richard's financial accomplishments. I think Mark is going to be in the fight of his life." With the mention of her son's name, Christina searches the standing crowd for his face.

"Poor kid! Hope he is okay. He went in earlier to take his place before the service. Oh, there he is. You can't miss him when he stands up!" They both smile and wait for him just outside the entrance. Just then, Christina notices a slightly built balding man close by chatting with James. She points them out to Jeanne. "Excuse me for a minute. I need to speak to him. He was Richard's financial broker and strangely enough has been appointed as the estate co-representative with Andrew, Richard's brother. I am not sure why Richard would have done something like that. He was not that close to him. He was just his broker. I'll be right back."

Christina darts across the unfamiliar crowd near her. The man she greets looks surprised. James hurriedly scampers off when he sees Christina approaching. Hand outstretched, she reaches towards the man saying, "Hello, Alain, just a quick hello and to say thank you, in advance, for your help. Please look after Mark in the next few weeks." Looking completely dumbfounded he holds her hand limply. Then stammers through an incoherent reply, "Oh, yes, hello Christina - fine, yes," and then quickly excuses himself.

Christina returns to where Jeanne is waiting. Her voice tinged with suspicion she looks at Jeanne saying, "That was really strange. Something is going on."

Jeanne looks at her with deep concern as she gestures with her chin at all the strange groupings around them. Papers are being passed from hand to hand and men are seen in huddled, whispering groups. "With the number of briefcases here today, I'm surprised they even waited for this final service."

Both women turn to look at Mark exiting the hall along with others. He is wearing a dapper, dark-blue suit. His face is expressionless as he works his way through the crowd. His large-shouldered frame towers above everyone else, his hazel eyes - his father's eyes, are piercing as he looks around for his mother.

Christina is approached by a small gray-haired woman whom she obviously knows. They hug and the woman asks her to step aside with her for a moment. Christina excuses herself from Jeanne again and the two move a little distance away. The newcomer, Anne, is peering at Christina through thick lenses. "I still can't believe they were not going to tell Mark his dad had died! They got a shock when Mark walked in here today, not only because he had the guts to be here, but because he looks so much like his father. At first I thought you should not come, but it is a good thing you did. I thought Monika would make a big scene if she saw you. You were always a threat to her."

"No, the sick thing is that Mark was her real threat. If it had not been for you – and your initial call, we would not even have known Richard had died. Thank you! Wait till I tell you more. That witch also managed to keep Mark from the viewing.

Do you know Richard's legs are missing? I will call you later and fill you in. I do need to speak to Andrew and try figure out what the hell is going on. Richard is probably shaking his head at the ridiculousness of this funeral. He did not deserve this."

Anne looks very serious as she reaches for something in her bag and then hands Christina some papers as discreetly as she can. Her voice is low as she says: "You need to look at this, Christina. Show it to Andrew when you start hiring attorneys."

"What do you mean, hiring attorneys?" Christina looks puzzled and Anne looks at her with sadness saying, "You are right, Richard did not deserve this. We will miss him and I know you will too. Bless you and Mark. Call me later. I hope you can visit the farm soon. You are always welcome." Anne leaves quickly, avoiding any further questions.

Christina is left clutching the papers and starts reading them as she walks back to Jeanne who now has Mark standing beside her. Jeanne has a comforting hand on his arm and is smiling proudly up at him.

Christina quickly folds the papers and stuffs them in her bag as she approaches them, having seen something on the pages that she may not want to share at that moment. Mark is telling Jeanne what happened to him when he first arrived at the service.

"When I got here, James had me moving chairs around, treating me as though I were nothing more than another gofer employee like him. Damn it! I am here to grieve for my father. Then, you won't believe this, but Monika thought she could cut me down to size by ordering me to sit at the back of the hall, refusing to allow me to sit with her sons in the front. Samantha stepped in. She was already in the front and told me to pull up a chair next to hers. So I pulled up a chair in the front!"

Christina's eyes are darting back and forth with anger. "Hold on, Mom. I know you. Don't even try finding her right now. It is just not worth it. She is not worth it! She does this stuff to get a reaction."

Jeanne smiles at the two of them. She obviously knows them well and defuses the situation by saying, "I think Mark has shown great strength. Who is Samantha by the way?"

Mark answers as he looks around. "She is my newly-found half sister from Canada. That reminds me, she told me about an after-party at Dad's house starting shortly."

Christina looks mortified. "What? You are not serious. Mark, they will treat you like dirt! They have no souls. You are the only thing standing between her and your father's money!"

"Mom, I am going! They don't scare me at all." Mark looks at her seriously as a passerby overhears him and says, "Christina, Mark, it is really good to see you again. I could not help overhearing that. I'll take Mark and stay with him. It would be my privilege. Richard was a very good friend and he would want his son to be there."

Mark answers quickly, "Great, thanks, Ted."

Christina nods to the man. "Thank you, Ted. That's very kind of you. Mark probably needs a man with him at the party."

The two of them walk away together. Mark looks back over his shoulder with a smile, saying, "Mom, call me and I will give you a party update."

She looks at the retreating men whilst reaching into her bag for the papers received from Anne earlier. "Ted was a good friend of Richard's and lives up our way. He chose not to socialize with the Miami bunch, so both may not be too welcome at the party." Christina opens the papers in her hands saying,

"I need to share something. I only managed to read the first few lines. So much for Richard's heart attack on the wave-runner!"

"***Water-Bike Crash Victim Bled to Death****. A Canadian man killed in a weekend water-scooter accident died of a torn aorta, an autopsy has found. Richard St. John's water-bike collided with one driven by his brother-in-law according to the Florida Marine Patrol. The brother-in-law walked away from the accident unharmed. Last year Monroe County led the State in water-bike accidents. The crafts have been increasingly controversial in the Keys....*"

The two women stand open-mouthed and motionless for a few minutes. Jeanne is the first to comment as she motions to the crowd around them. "I think we should head back. We can chat more privately in the car. "

Christina notices that they have attracted the attention from others around them who seem to have an interest in their conversation. Numerous funeral-goers have moved closer. "Well, now you know why I was worried about Mark going to this party. He could be the next victim!"

They head toward the SUV still chatting in quiet

undertones. Christina's voice is strained. "Well, wasn't that perfect! I really hope Richard did not see it coming. That would have been more hurtful to him than the wave-runner impact itself." Christina's last comment obviously makes her emotional and her eyes well-up with tears.

Once again Jeanne summons comforting words that remind Christina of her role as mother and protector. Her tears turn to determined planning. "It was probably very quick, dear, but I do think you need to get hold of the Florida Marine Patrol mentioned in this report and the sheriff's office. Remember, my husband is ex-FBI. I'll tell him about this, and we will help in any way we can." Christina is driving and glances briefly at Jeanne sitting next to her.

"Thank you, Jeanne. We may need his help. I will call the Florida Marine Patrol first thing. I also need to call Andrew, Richard's brother. He was a homicide detective in Canada, you know. I wonder what he thinks. Maybe that's why he said nothing at the funeral. I will see this through to the very end. Richard always said I was pigheaded."

Jeanne responds with a brief laugh and then turns in her

seat to face Christina. Her voice is filled with concern. "I have a feeling Mark is in for a long battle. When my own father died we were flung into a bitter family feud with his new gold-digger wife. Then once I got rid of her by paying her off, the attorneys took the rest! This doesn't have to happen here. Monika and her gang have no idea of the strength of character and courage you both have." She gently touches the back of Christina's long blond hair, adding, "Besides, you have the loyalty of your friends. Something Monika probably doesn't have, not when it comes to money. They are all going to be in it for themselves."

Christina feels a rippling body shiver in response to Jeanne's touch. "Thank you so much for coming with us today. This wasn't something Mark and I could have faced alone. Can you call Mark for me? I don't like to use my cell while driving." Jeanne nods and reaches into her handbag for her cell phone. She repeats the number Christina gives her as she dials. As she chats with Mark, she repeats much of the conversation for Christina. "What? They are asking a lot of questions. Like - is Ted your attorney or bodyguard? Strange questions to be asking after a funeral, don't you think? Well, be careful Mark. Yes, I know you can take care of yourself. Okay, then I will tell Mom you are fine. What's that? Yes, I can hear the lightning and you are breaking up a little. Always best to get off the phone in a lightning storm. Bye for now."

She looks across at Christina and in a serious, monotone voice says, "Did you hear those crazy questions about Ted? He also said that Monika is not grieving at all but behaving like the perfect, smiling party hostess. I don't know how to say this, but I truly believe you may discover Richard was murdered."

Christina's knuckles are clenched white around the steering wheel. She nods a response to Jeanne and repeats the words from the newspaper clipping, "... *impact that caused internal trauma and bleeding*. Probably the reason for his swollen chest and why he had no legs - probably murder. It's all beginning to fall into place. Luckily Mark was not with him on the wave-runner this time."

The breeze blowing across the African plains is gently rustling the tall golden Savannah grass. Soon the breeze changes into gusts of wind. The grass parts intermittently to expose a

troop of monkeys scampering for the cover of a nearby tree. They know that the change means an approaching storm.

The statuesque leopard perched on a rock watching them is sniffing the air and just as quickly climbs off the rock. Christina had her camera lens trained on the leopard as she asks. " Where did she go?"

Mark's quick reply is tinged with excitement. "Look Mom. The leopard had two baby cubs hiding in the grass. She is carrying them in her mouth just like our cat Misty carried her kittens."

Christina and Mark are with the game ranger in the open-back jeep. They all feel the wind and fine droplets of rain on their skin. The game ranger leaps into action jumping out of the jeep to put up the vehicle's roof. Mark makes every effort as a nine-year old to help, jumping off too. Just as quickly both the game ranger and Christina are pulling him back on the jeep by the back of his shirt collar. They hoist him back into the jeep. The game ranger speaks first. "Oh no you don't young man - you want to be leopard food."

Christina follows this with, "Lucky the leopard has a mouthful or, it could have been you or the monkeys."

Mark looks at them both as he feels the back of his shirt collar. " Yes, and you pulled me up just like the leopard did to her cubs - by the scruff of my neck."

They all laugh as they drive off ahead of the storm as the game ranger says, " Yes, all about timing. The leopard had been watching that troop of baboons waiting for her moment to pounce. Lucky for the monkeys that the storm came."

Christina smiles at Mark's almost inaudible and spiritual words over the jeep's loud engine. "God sends the storms to clean the air and heal the earth."

a welcome death...

Chapter FIVE

The Key Largo hotel café has the mixed remnants of a seated breakfast and an incoming lunch crowd. The room has a pale green hue from the reflected sunlight on the painted walls. White bamboo chairs with floral green and pink seat cushions match the table overlays. There is a low hum of chatter with the strains of ambient music filtering through the room. Christina and Mark are seated near the doorway and their occasional glances toward the open door bear evidence of an expected meeting. They eat and chat intermittently. In the weeks since Richard's death, they have researched every aspect of the accident. They have interviewed everyone who was willing to talk to them. Their efforts and analytical late-night talks have turned them into a team. They are ready for anything.

A uniformed, sandy-haired marine patrolman enters the doorway with a sense of purpose. His appearance is that of an adult Boy Scout due to an awkward combination of uniform shorts, muscular tanned legs covered in curly blond hair and a baseball cap pulled tightly down on his head, the peak casting a slight shadow over sky-blue eyes and strong jaw line. He strides over to Christina and Mark, who are both looking directly at him. Christina waves to him in vague acknowledgment. With handshakes all around, Investigator Chip Hogan joins their table. He rests his sun-tanned forearms on the table and looks at Mark piercingly, remarking he needn't have worried about recognizing them - Mark looks exactly like his father. Mark grins, as Christina delivers a well-rehearsed, "He is a clone of his father in almost every way."

The patrolman attempts a strained smile and repeats the observation. "Yes, you look very much like your father. I am very sorry. Please accept my condolences…"

Christina tries to hide the impatience in her voice as she interrupts the rest of his statement. "Investigator Hogan, we felt it necessary to see you to fully understand what happened to Richard and to see where he died."

"Sure thing. After we talk you can follow my truck to the beach area close to where the accident occurred. Let me also say right now that nothing, I mean nothing, is going to change my mind that this was anything but an accident!" Christina and Mark look startled at his predetermined statement and his defensive attitude.

Mark's curt reply surprises the patrolman. "Perhaps we should say collision at this point. How can you be so sure it was an accident?"

Hogan's reply is firm. "Unless you can offer me any further evidence right now, I believe it was an accident. I am going by the witness and crash reports." Mark continues with matching firmness. "What witnesses? My father is dead and the only two witnesses were the two involved with the collision and his death - Avi and Kenny. Please explain the collision then."

The patrolman looks a little unnerved but begins his tale that bears all the language of an official report. "The accident occurred when Kenny Levin, Mr. St. John's brother-in-law, collided with him in a zigzag maneuver. Levin said he was not sure if this was accidental, or if they each misunderstood the intention of the other, or if St. John was starting a zigzag-type game. Your father's actual cause of death according to the report was from a ruptured aorta and broken back. You are right, there was another person, Avi Shalev, who was part of the Jet Ski group, but he declared he was not there at impact."

Christina has noticed Mark's pained face and interrupts with some reassurance in her voice. It is clear that she is hoping Investigator Hogan will take her lead and approach this with more sensitivity. Her next words and the fact that she addresses him by his first name may be an effort to disarm him, or it may mean that she has lost respect for his official role. "Chip, I am sure he could not have suffered, if it was so sudden."

The patrolman's answer is directed at her and is obviously intentional in its insensitivity. "Although it was a sudden accident, it must have been a slow death. He must have suffered." Investigator Hogan's expanded chest and stiffened shoulders show the defensive nature of his mounting hostility.

Christina is clearly fighting her rising anger. She is crossing and uncrossing her legs, as well as shifting back and forth in her seat. The two men remain in a fixed stance. She is perturbed at the investigator's prevailing hostility toward them, possibly based on prior negative assumptions about mother and son and their role here. She is trying hard to conduct this meeting with as much grace as possible, trying not to offend the man or dent his blatant ego as she continues, “We need to know if you think there is anything, anything at all suspicious?”

His reply is swift. “Once again, let me tell you. Nothing will convince me this was anything else but a…” Christina is now showing annoyance as she finishes his sentence, “Accident! I know, you already said that.”

Hogan looks at her with disdain. He continues with pride in his voice, “In fact, I am going to be using this accident in a seminar next week. Jet skis, wave-runners, whatever anyone wants to call them, these devices are very dangerous, especially if you do not know what you are doing, or are fooling around.”

This time Mark interrupts. His usually warm-toned voice level is raised and he is scowling at the patrolman. “My father was very adept at water sports. He taught me to be extremely cautious on the water. Besides, considering the fact that wave-runners are so disliked and even banned in this area, isn't this a great way to engineer a fatal incident and avoid suspicion?”

Christina leans closer to her son, showing her support. Hogan is now fidgeting with his belted hip radio and looks at

Mark with concern, replying, "There was nothing to make me think it was more than an accident. In fact, Ken Levin was obviously in a state of shock afterward and even said, 'Why did it have to be Richard? He has no enemies."

The side of Mark's lip curls as he grits his teeth, saying, "And you don't think that was a strange thing to say if it was only an accident? Perhaps even a little *too* defensive?"

Hogan looks at them blankly, turning his head to look at Christina, who continues, "What nonsense! He was a wealthy, powerful man with as many enemies as friends worldwide. He always had some feud or business litigation going on."

Chip Hogan looks startled at these assertions. They seem to be swaying his prior determined resolve. His next statement is more subdued. "My job is to identify accidents and control the waters, as well as monitor fish and wildlife. I believe this was an accident. I have never investigated a possible homicide. In fact, I have no training or experience in that area."

Christina is alerted by these last words of honesty and is no longer shifting in her seat. "Okay, so you mean, even if it was a possible homicide, you may not have recognized it?"

Hogan's reply comes as he pushes his seat back noisily and crosses his arms defensively over his chest. "If it was a homicide I did not recognize it, and there was nothing to make me believe it was more than an accident."

Christina and Mark look at each other in disbelief and with an element of amazement as she reaches down into her bag next to the chair. Her hair sweeps the top of the table with the movement. Hogan looks at the pages she takes out of the bag with some apprehension. She holds the sheets of paper in both hands, elbows resting on the table. She looks at the patrolman, glancing at the badge on his chest, says, "Investigator Hogan, do you know there are two wills that have surfaced, both of which we are told could be forged, and that Richard was a very wealthy man and a diplomat - the Consul General of Liberia for Canada? Through the efforts of a good friend, we have had an FBI handwriting analyst look at these and he is positive they were not signed by Richard, especially as he was left-handed. These wills and the initials on each page, we believe, do not bear his real signature. Also, there was a recent one-million-dollar insurance policy naming his new wife, Monika, as the sole beneficiary.

The morning after Richard died, Monika managed to track down the insurance agent vacationing in another state to lay claim to the money. She did not even wait for the viewing or funeral to be over. Richard was barely cold!"

Mark continues. "The group around my father did not tell me my father had died. We had to hear it from a friend. They were hoping to probate one of these fake wills before I found out. In fact, when we did find out, we were told he died of a heart attack. There was no mention of any collision."

Mark then points to one of the pages and continues, "This will was sent anonymously to our attorneys from my father's office. Our challenge is to find the original, which may have been destroyed. Apparently, the day after his death, two of the people in my father's office went through all his papers and then spent a couple of hours behind closed doors, together with Monika. We believe this is when they forged this will."

Mark leans forward, fingering through the pages in the patrolman's hands and pulls some stapled sheets out, "I mean, look at this one. They are claiming this is the *real* one. I got this copy from my Uncle Andrew. It has spelling mistakes and has a crooked paragraph that looks pasted in. It makes reference to the female word, testatrix and not testator. How Freudian! There are two male personal representatives named in the will. They obviously were thinking of Monika when they wrote that!"

Christina offers a supportive statement. "Richard was a very smart and thorough businessman. He would never have signed a will full of mistakes or looking so sloppy! I have hundreds of legal documents with his signature and these are not his signatures! We were only told about the will benefiting the new wife after the funeral, by Andrew, Richard's brother. It leaves everything to Monika. Impossible! It is dated prior to the death of Richard's mother, Mark's grandmother. Richard loved his mother. He would never have cut his mother out. He was supporting her in a nursing home. And the will named Alain du Pont, almost a complete stranger, one of Richard's stockbrokers, as the co-representative with Richard's brother. Definitely not something Richard would have done. In fact, Alain withdrew when he found out. I was not surprised!"

She looks at Mark and says, "That was probably why Alain was so nervous when I went to say hello to him at the funeral. He was even more surprised when I asked him to take care of you through all of this. That may have been the reason he backed off. They might have named him because your dad had a substantial amount of money at his firm and they wanted to be sure they laid their hands on it."

Looking back at Hogan, she continues, "Did you know there is an extensive prenuptial agreement leaving Monika practically nothing? They were married only a year … and she actually thinks she should be entitled to Richard's entire estate! We are going to subpoena it."

The patrolman's bravado has been replaced by a look of startled concern. Christina looks at his face and recognizing his increased attention adds, "There is the chance Richard may not have even been in Florida when he was supposed to have signed this will." She points at the date. "We are going to research the paper trail. He was probably in Toronto en route to his niece's twenty-first birthday celebration. Obviously, we can only do this once we have access to Richard's office papers, and Monika is claiming they have disappeared. They are supposed to be in Andrew's hands as the estate representative."

Chip Hogan's shoulders are hunched over. He leans forward, shifting his chair closer to the table, putting the papers down and sliding them toward Christina. She shifts them back directly in front of the patrolman. He reluctantly picks them up again, forearms on the table. He looks at the documentation blankly, murmuring, "His jet skis were so old. That didn't say money. If I had known some of this at the time, perhaps I would have looked at things a little differently."

Mark and Christina smile at each other knowingly. Their eyes acknowledge his simple deduction. Christina answers the point. "I'm not surprised the jet skis were old, because Richard was somewhat eccentric and could be very cheap at times, and on other occasions extremely extravagant."

Chip Hogan nods in agreement. "That could be. I have some rich friends who behave like that too." He continues very defensively saying, "I must tell you that all standard procedures were followed. I made sure of that. Of course he had his autopsy. It's regulation, you know. I insisted on the autopsy even though his wife was vehemently against it. I even made sure that the Jet Skis were photographed."

He is fingering the wills as Christina reaches back into her bag. He watches her with apprehension and exhales through his teeth.

Christina places some newspaper articles on top of the papers in his hands, saying, "I am sure she did not want an autopsy and not because of her religion! These are newspaper clippings showing that Richard was not only very wealthy, but also described as an international tycoon, Consul General of Liberia in Canada and a prominent member of society. I mean, it could have been anything - a hit from Liberia or, his new wife!"

It is evident that the patrolman is still pondering the wills as he asks, "Well, I am not sure about all of that. Who are the estate benefactors?" Christina replies, "That's just it. One will names only Monika, which is ridiculous, since he loved his son and his mother. At the time of his death he was still supporting his mother in Canada. The other will arrived via Canada from his brother, but had been postmarked from Richard's office area. It certainly appears to be a will that Richard could have executed as far as the correct spelling and legal usage. But, besides the content, the signature is still a little odd and has been described as a possible forgery by our FBI contact. Even more disturbing is the cover letter found in the envelope. That's what really raised our suspicions." She pulls it from the pile in his hands. "We don't know who wrote this," she says and reads it aloud. *"Richard was a good friend and I will miss him. I went to great lengths to lay my hands on this, Richard's true will. Please ensure his wishes are carried out. I have sent the original to Richard's brother with copies to the firms of attorney..."*

Investigator Hogan stares intently at the papers. He is muttering almost inaudibly, "So that is why they did not want St. John to have an autopsy. They said he was Jewish as well."

Christina is startled. She reaches for her left eyelid in annoyance. Rubbing the eye she says, "Excuse me? What did you say? Sorry, my left eyelid twitches whenever I am tired or stressed. My mother used to say it meant I was going to have a fight. Investigator Hogan, you said they did not want an autopsy because Richard was Jewish too. Wow! She tried every trick in the book. You obviously found out Richard was Catholic? She really has no soul. She does not behave anything like the Jewish people I know. They usually care deeply about family."

Hogan looks surprised and blurts out. "Oh, he had his autopsy, I told you that. It's regulation, you know. I insisted on it, and I did find out he was Catholic. As I said, all the correct regulations were followed. We processed everything. The jet skis were photographed. I am going to ask Mark to look at the photos to identify which scratches may have been there before. The actual jet skis were taken by their owner, Mrs. St. John. Sorry, I mean, the other Mrs. St. John."

Mark nods. "I know exactly which scratches were on the jet skis. I was on them often with him. By the way, they are my father's property, not hers. She is not the rightful owner."

Hogan takes a deep breath before continuing. "The jet skis were then later left on the side of the highway, I-95. They claimed the trailer hitch broke and then when they went back for them, the trailer and jet skis had disappeared. These wills could have been forged after the accident. I had no idea! I wish I had known some of this at the time."

Christina is looking aghast at Hogan. "You mean the only physical evidence has been left on the side of I-95? How convenient! Do you know where they are now?"

"I think they were reported to the road patrol for being on the side of the road and maybe stolen. I do not know where they are now." Hogan is stammering. He keeps glancing at the newspaper clippings and looks very distressed.

Christina reaches into her bag again, placing one more page carefully on the table between them. "If you speak to any of Richard's friends listed here you may uncover some motives. You are free to ask them about our relationship, which they will be honest enough to verify was troubled, but I am sure they will also tell you Richard loved his mother and son very much. They may or, may not also tell you that Richard and Monika were having marital problems, usually about money and his wanting to see his son. Quite bizarre! We have been told by one of them, that's his contact number." Christina points a well-manicured finger at the list before continuing. "Monika may have been having an affair with Avi, a former Israeli commander. There is a question of whether he was, or was not present at the crash site. Conflicting reports from Avi himself are floating around. It's also been said that this may have been a hit by the rumored Israeli Mafia in Miami. Do you think this really exists?"

Hogan replies quickly, “Oh, yes! My wife is Jewish; I’ve heard of them. On the other side of the coin, Kenny Levin told me Richard had marital problems with his ex-wife. That would be you, I assume. I have an ex-wife too. I gather that Richard did not get on with his own brothers, as well.”

Christina glares at him. She buries a sarcastic laugh in her reply. “Investigator Hogan, I am sure the Miami group has said many things to cover their bases, especially in preparation for this meeting. During her brief marriage Monika tried everything she could to destroy the relationship between Richard and Mark, as well as between any of his brothers who may have threatened her inheritance. Even more especially right now. God forbid she may have to share her new-found wealth, Richard’s wealth! She apparently floated around at the after-funeral party as the perfect smiling hostess, with no tears. She even cruelly denied a request from Richard’s brother, Andrew at this party for a family photo he saw of himself with Richard on a shelf. What never failed to surprise me, as well as others was how Monika’s former husband managed to stay friends with both of them, considering it was Richard who broke up that marriage. She was a married woman when Richard met her, and her children often told Mark that his father was 'good for the money.' She showed no scruples from the beginning and her financial intentions were always very clear. When I divorced Richard I told him to stick his money but that I expected him to take care of his son. I agreed to only receive a few hundred dollars a month for Mark, no alimony for myself even though I helped him in many of his businesses. I was tired of the control factor via his money. He always assured me that Mark was the only benefactor of his estate. He was a millionaire and then used that monthly stipend to try to control us! I am sure you understand divorce, but would you cut your divorced children out of your will? Or, your own mother for that matter?"

Hogan's reply is swift. "Of course not, I love them." Christina continues, "Exactly! The fact of the matter is, not only did Richard love his son and want the best for him, but also he loved his mother and brothers deeply. Yes, the three brothers argued occasionally like any siblings do. Yes, they were a little jealous of Richard as the baby who seemed to turn every business deal he had into gold. From his side he truly loved them and was even trying to help Andrew and his family make the move to Florida to be closer to him."

Hogan looks embarrassed. He glances down at the table, folds the papers firmly and gestures toward his watch. "Thank you for the information. We'd better get going if you want to see where the accident occurred. Follow me, my truck is up front."

Mark and Christina stand simultaneously. They look relieved at the patrolman's new shift in attitude, as well as the proposed break in conversation. They follow the patrolman out of the restaurant. Before he leaps into his truck, he extends an arm in the direction he wants them to take. Mother and son are quick to follow his lead. The SUV follows closely behind the patrolman's truck to a beach area a few miles north of the hotel.

Hogan is standing on the beach and pointing out to sea as Mark and Christina approach him. She raises her hand over her eyes to protect them from the glare as well as to try to hide tears welling up in her eyes. Her long skirt blows in the ocean breeze to expose her sandaled feet. Mark's long neck is cocked thoughtfully to the side. His keen hazel eyes peer out to sea. His denim-clad legs are firmly parted. His hands are in his pockets, his sneakers squarely planted in the beach sand. Composed, Mark speaks first. “From what you are saying, the collision occurred fairly far out. Nobody would have seen anything from the shore. No witnesses?”

The patrolman replies, “There was a pontoon boat that came upon the scene after it happened and they did try to revive him. Ken, the brother-in-law said he tried to get Richard onto the back of his wave-runner, but he kept slipping off because of his size and unconscious state. When our patrol boat got there they tried CPR as well.”

He grimaces as he continues. “In fact, my colleague at the scene said Richard vomited all over his uniform.”

Christina is standing behind him. She grimaces and shakes her head in response to his last callous comment. She glances over at Mark with concern and he in turn looks away at that point.

Mark turns to look directly at the patrolman and is the next to speak. “But they didn't see it happen?”

The patrolman looks briefly down at his boots embedded in the beach sand as he says, “No.”

Mark is showing his new-found confidence and bravely asks, "At the viewing my mother and I saw that my father had lost his legs. What happened to them?"

Hogan turns to Christina, who had been standing a little behind them listening intently but fighting back her tears. The patrolman has noticed. His reply is tinged with sympathy. "I am not quite sure but I believe they harvested his long bones as a registered organ donor."

Mark's next statement is quick: "When your report is finalized I would like a copy."

Hogan glances up at Mark who stands a good head and shoulders above him. "Sure, as soon as I get it done. At this point it is still an open investigation. I will keep it open until we have all the evidence." Both Mark and Christina reply to this with genuine thanks.

Christina has her stoic self back and asks, "Where was Monika after the accident?"

Hogan looks at her and says, "I was told that she did not want to see him like that and refused to go to the accident scene. Instead, she went to the hospital and waited to hear the news."

Christina continues with anger, “So, she never wanted to be near him or with him at the end? What a loving wife! Then she orders his cremation and a plastic urn! Damn her! She is going to have some *real* karma to deal with!” Mark stands silent. He knows there is no stopping Christina as she continues, enraged, “Why the cover-ups and lies if you have nothing to hide? You know what my mother heard from a friend in South Africa? That Monika has claimed that Richard died in a rollover car accident - and that she and her two boys were the only survivors! Talk about a parallel-reality version of the facts!”

Hogan decides to shift the situation and begins to walk toward his truck saying, “I will get those photos and let Mark take a look.” He walks past Christina first and as he does whispers, “Don’t worry. I will not show him the photographs of his father.” She whispers back an inaudible, “Thank you.”

Hogan turns to look at Mark and says, "Mark, follow me to the truck and we can look at the wave-runner photos.”

The patrolman’s scrunching boots are heard solidly on the beach sand as they two men move away. They are soon standing at the truck, fingering and pointing at photos.

Christina walks to the water's edge. She looks pensively at the ocean and turns her head into the light sea breeze, which blows her long blond hair back from her fine-boned shoulders. Tears stream down her face as she gazes at the blue-green water where Richard died and perhaps left his last earthly energy. She whispers softly, "I know you can hear me and you know how much we loved you. We will fight for justice. Guide and make your son strong now." Christina turns away. She takes one last look out to sea over her shoulder before slowly heading back toward Mark and the patrolman who are still discussing the photos. She gets close to them, but stands a little apart, allowing her son to handle the moment.

Mark scoops up the photos, walking toward her, he says, "Mom, there are absolutely no new scrapes on the wave-runner, other than the one small one which was caused when I was with him. We scraped the side of the dock. There is not even any sort of bump that would have been caused by the kind of collision described by Kenny." Mark is showing the photos to his mother.

The patrolman adds to this, "I'll definitely look into this further. Ken Levin's a slight, frail man, and was pretty shaken up at the time. I am not sure how he could have been involved in something like this. It is interesting that he had absolutely no injuries himself. Not even a bruise."

Christina replies, "They definitely chose the right one to leave behind with Richard. No one would suspect someone like Kenny could be involved in Richard's death!"

Mark shuffles the photos into a pile in his hands and then hands them to Hogan, who prepares to leave the scene. "I need to get back to the station. I intend adding your comments to my report." The two men flip through the photographs one more time. Then the patrolman puts out his hand to shake theirs.

Mother and son look at the man with a rising sense of respect and Hogan shows a new sense of awareness as he leaves. Christina and Mark are left standing on the beach and they both walk closer to the water's edge. Mark is the first one to speak after their brief relieved silence.

"Are you okay, Mom?" She replies with a reassuring smile. "Yes, just in shock and I suppose relieved that it is over. Can't help looking at you and realizing you are all your father has left in this world and how children immortalize the man.

Whether or not we liked each other as divorced parents, he really was an incredible man and I will miss him."

"I know. I think that went well. Although it didn't start off too well. That Miami crowd really prepped him with BS. I hope Hogan gets to the bottom of this. I think he initially classified this as just another family estate battle."

Christina looks thoughtfully out to sea as she says, "You know what? Perhaps this location was chosen due to the fact that Monroe County is the leader in the state of Florida for wave-runner accidents. One more 'accident' would not draw too much attention... I am worried that the investigation may very well have been botched and that it's too late for the detectives to try to retrieve any evidence. Hogan himself may become concerned about possible litigation or retribution from us and start back-pedaling. He may not realize our intentions are genuine and that we really want justice. I believe Andrew wants that, too. I tell you what though, I am really happy you were not with your father on the wave-runner."

Mark laughs sarcastically. "I have no doubt that would have been Monika's plan before she realized she could not manipulate me on my weekends with them. That was when she really changed and started telling him stupid made-up stories about me. She just never realized he didn't believe her and instead starting meeting me quietly to keep the peace."

Christina shakes her head in disbelief. "Still can't figure out why he was so scared of her. She is such a tiny, silly woman. I wish he had married Beverly. She would have been a great stepmother to you. Your father never knew we had met Beverly when I first arrived in Florida. I really liked her. She was so funny and absolutely gorgeous. It is strange how I never wanted to meet Monika. Perhaps my soul knew her destiny path."

Mark smiles at his mother as they turn to leave. "I wish he had married Beverly, too. I got on with her. I think she really loved Dad and that's why she wouldn't put up with his womanizing. Monika's ego wouldn't allow her to believe Dad could ever want any other woman. Everyone was scared of her! Really, Mom, she has a nasty mouth. The confusing thing is that everyone says Monika is a mini version of you. She does have a similar look." Christina looks horrified and says, "Oh, God, no, don't say that!"

Christina's left eyebrow is raised, her lips tighten and her frown shows the seriousness of her next statement. "Do you remember what Magda, the psychic in South Africa, told us almost eight years ago? She said your father would die tragically one day, not by his own hand and not by accident. He would be surrounded in death by a conspiracy of many enemies. She saw a boating-type accident. I thought it could end up being an accident on his boat but never thought of his wave-runners. Well, I called her yesterday to tell her what happened."

Mark looks at her quizzically. "Why didn't you tell me that yesterday?"

Christina responds quickly. "Sorry, forgot to tell you that. She apologized for the sad outcome of her prediction. Remember she really does not like giving people bad news. Her exact words were, 'There will be many *snakes in the grass waiting to strike* and you are going to have to be as pigheaded as you can possibly be and see this through to the very end!' At that point a cold shiver went down my spine. You know what your father used to call me? Pigheaded! This is not a word Magda would ever use. She is a soft-spoken Polish immigrant. This word is the furthest thing from her vocabulary."

Mark's interest is piqued. "What else did she say?"

"She says we are in for the battle of our lives. She sees a similar end for Monika as she saw for Richard, with the same conspiring enemies. Now, you know we always need to practice doubt of any psychic prediction, but it is uncanny."

Lake Malawi was tranquil in the blue tones of a morning sunrise. Singing is heard in the distance as a group of young village girls coming from a ceremony and are making there way along the bank of the lake. They are being followed by a scampering group of even younger children.

Christina is sitting with her two-year old son Mark on the trunk of a fallen tree. She had just placed her camera down since it was apparently it was scaring the group. Christina was not sure why this was happening, or if they perhaps thought this was some other kind of device. Every time she held it to her eye on the camera to focus - the group would dive into the fine, white sand. Then as she put the camera down, they would stand up and begin singing again. Christina made two attempts and then placed the camera on the tree trunk to enjoy the sights and sounds with her son. So, when a little boy wearing only a small loin wrap darted from the group and ran up to them she thought he might be curious about the camera. However, to her astonishment the little boy put his tiny hands directly into her long blond hair and tugged. Christina lifted him onto the log with them and allowed him to play with her hair that he seemed completely intrigued with. Mark immediately wanted to play too, so she had both boys pulling on her hair. The ceremonial group was undeterred and continued their walk to the edge of the lake.

The Lake lodge owner was laughing aloud as he approached the threesome on the tree trunk. "The Pikininny (young black boy) has obviously never seen long blond hair before. The village behind that hill is very remote. He might be trying to see if it is straw. Usually their ceremonial members have straw on their heads as part of the masks. That group over there is doing their Virgin Maiden ceremony so one of them is probably going to be married soon. Come along...we are serving breakfast. Richard is 'wheeling and dealing' with another guest from Sweden."

Christina laughs with him as she peers through her hair which has now been pulled over her face.

"This trip has truly been an incredible. I am grateful Richard agreed to our meeting in Malawi this time. We always have to find a good meeting place between South Africa and Canada for him to see Mark. Not to sound pretentious, but usually it is somewhere in Europe because of his international business travels. This has been a great experience and just what the doctor ordered for all of us."

Then, quite suddenly the young boy recognizing that the energy has shifted from play to departure, lets her hair go, giggles, and runs back to his group - waving goodbye to his new-found friends.

Both Christina and Mark smile and wave back before Christina lifts Mark onto her hip. She then proceeds to brush off the white sand from his bare feet with her hand. She places the strap of the camera around her neck and they follow the khaki-clad man along the small, winding trail back to the lodge. Mark is happily bouncing on his mother's hip.

Quite suddenly, a few feet ahead, a long black snake slithers across the path. The man's bush boots stop abruptly in the dirt. He speaks quietly. "Careful... a snake won't bother you if you don't bother it."

Christina responds in a whisper. "Yes, I know part of my upbringing was on a farm in South Africa, so I have experienced many snakes. I am more frightened of the human variety crossing my path. They are the unpredictable kind!"

Smiles follow but no fear is shown from their brief snake encounter as they proceed.

for a broken soul…

Chapter SIX

Large African masks and an ornately-framed oil painting of a lioness with her cub watch over Christina from the cream walls of her Florida home office. She is seated at a large light-oak desk, her blond hair tightly pulled back in a ponytail from her troubled, tanned face. Her left elbow leans on the desk and she cradles her head with her left hand. Her right wrist bearing a gold Cartier bangle is resting on a notepad. With a pen at the ready, she starts creating a time line of events.

She is occasionally distracted by palm fronds blown against the open window. Afternoon noises of passing cars and children playing outside drift through her thoughts. She is reviewing the marine patrol and witness reports.

Perplexed, she is looking at the documents in front of her when Mark's footsteps on the hardwood floor make her look up. He smiles at her as he walks into the sunlit room then flops into the corner leopard-print armchair saying: "None of it makes any sense, does it?"

She shakes her head and places the back of the pen between her teeth, replying through the clenched grip, "I don't know how many times you went through this, but this is my sixth attempt at trying to reconstruct a time line. It's such a farce, and looking at the damage to your father's body in such clinical terms is really awful!"

He replies swiftly, "I know!" Changing the subject he adds, "It's nice to have a window open for a change - instead of the air conditioner." He looks toward the window, trying to hide the pain in his eyes from his mother's gaze. She notices the light catching the shine of possible tears and immediately changes the subject to the task at hand.

"Okay, here we go. Look at the accident witness statements. My God! Note number one is a description of the location, and forms part of an Internet Marine Patrol Accident Investigation report. Now, listen to this."

Christina reads from the top page. "*St. John's water-bike collided with another driven by his brother-in-law, Kenneth Levin. The two were crisscrossing in Blackwater Sound off the Island's bay side, according to Florida Marine Officer, Hogan.*

Last year, Monroe County led the State in water-bike accidents. These water-bikes are known by their brand name Jet Ski. They have drawn the ire of Keys residents. Earlier this year they were banned in 11 spots up and down the island chain. St. John was not in one of these spots."

Mark has his head back on the chair. His hazel eyes, glazed in thought, watch Christina as he listens intently. She continues reading, glancing up at him between file notes to see his reaction. "Note number two is Kenny Levin's on-site evidence and the interpretation by the marine patrolman. *Vessel #1 was being operated by Kenneth Levin, Vessel #2 by Richard St. John. According to Mr. Levin, they were cruising toward a marina. Mr. Levin was to port and Mr. St. John to starboard traveling in a North East direction. Levin stated that both vessels impacted, ejecting both operatives...."*

Mark suddenly stands, still dressed in his preppy school uniform of khaki slacks and green polo shirt. He leans over the desk and picks up the notepad. Then gently takes the pen out of his mother's inactive hand, saying, "While you read, I am going to try and sketch the accident scene from the witness reports.

Then we can compare it to the drawing in the Marine Patrol report. Right now it makes absolutely no sense and maybe my sketch will help."

Mark flops back down and starts sketching the scene on the notepad resting on his knee.

Christina continues reading intently. "Now, this is where it gets very confusing. Note number three is Avi's actual on-scene witness statement to the Marine Patrol. *Myself, Kenny and Richard were riding Jet Skis. I left them alone for about 15 to 20 minutes. When I came back with my dog on my jet ski I found Richard and Kenny already in the water.* But I thought Kenny's statement said all three of them were there at the time?"

Mark looks up at her saying, "Exactly! Now read Kenny's account. The next note, I think it's # 4…"

Christina reads the page in response: "Yes, *Note #4 ... the accident happened when we were all coming back to the beach, with Avi riding in front.* Now, this completely contradicts Avi's report. He said he had left them alone for 15 to 20 minutes and it happened while he was away. How can Marine Patrol not have picked up on this?"

They look at each other in disbelief. Mark shifts his frame in the armchair, leaning to one side, dumbfounded, as he says, “They completely contradict each other. Kenny says all three of them were there and Avi says he was not there. I wonder who is lying!”

Christina looks back at the report, picks it up and leans in her leather office chair in a similar sideways posture in agreement with her son’s. She winces a little and her hand squeezes her forehead. She reads the next few lines with emphasis on some of the words. “It gets even more contradictory in Kenny’s next few lines. Listen to this: ‘*We ALL seemed to be going in the same direction. Richard’s Jet Ski had been stalling and we crossed each other and the jet skis clipped each other. At that point I saw nothing else.’* Talk about conflicting witnesses. And this is meant to be a true story! What was this investigator thinking?”

Mark looks up abruptly from the notepad that he is doodling on, and with a flabbergasted but concerned look on his face shakes his head. “I can’t believe the Marine Patrol actually accepted the conflicting witness stories! Are you okay, Mom?”

“Oh, it’s just one of those damn headaches starting again. I am really getting tired of dealing with them.”

Christina lunges into her next observation without taking a breath. “What about the fact that Kenny's report says the two machines only clipped each other? Surely that sort of impact would not be hard enough to catapult them both into the water? Or, for that matter, cause such bad bodily damage - I mean, look at the autopsy report in here - or, no, perhaps you shouldn't. There is a note here that the blood toxicology report is still being finalized. Did I tell you I spoke to Barbara about the autopsy? You know she also works as a trauma doctor, not only as a GP? Well, she says there is absolutely no way this happened just from falling off the wave-runner. They must have hit him in the water to have broken his back and ripped his aorta off his heart.”

Mark's face shows his emotion as he quickly changes the conversation back to the crash scene. “As far as the crash is concerned, it is obvious they are covering up facts. Why, for example, did Dad have two catches of his jacket undone? Perhaps he was in the water by that stage and saw someone about to run him over and he tried to dive and couldn’t get out of the way in time. The extensive body damage can be explained that way."

Christina turns her gaze downward in response to Mark's brave attempt to mention his father's damaged body and says in a low voice tinged with anger, "It does not take a rocket scientist to know that someone is lying - the Marine Patrol screwed up royally! The fact that either Kenny or Avi may have worked on your father's jet ski the night before never even comes up. Wasn't one of them a mechanic? They would know exactly how to cause a problem with the machine. This could have caused the machine's stalling. Someone could have intentionally damaged it. Do we know for a fact that Avi was having an affair with Monika, or is this just a rumor?"

Christina slams a fist on her desk in frustration and an empty water glass bounces off, breaking on the wooden floor as she says, "Damn it! How could they all just ignore the possibility it could be murder?"

Mark slowly gets up from his seated position and bends down, picking up the shattered glass. Christina does the same and they pool the pieces into a folder from the desk, as Mark continues with a note of sarcasm, “Okay, that’s the end of my artist’s sketch - impossible if there are completely different eyewitness accounts. We need to carry on with this and take it to the next level with the FBI. We need to hire attorneys.”

Christina sits back down and says, “We obviously need to take this to Chip Hogan’s superiors. He has not been taking my calls since we met. We were lucky enough to get this Marine Patrol report and autopsy document out of him. I'll dictate and you put it into the computer.”

Mark smiles as he stands up and moves toward the computer desk, complaining, “Me and my big mouth!”

Christina dictates from her notepad as she sorts through the numerous documents, adding necessary quotations. Mark sits upright at the computer. He is obviously adept and finishes almost before his mother completes sentences. She remarks, “You know, your father was always amazed at your stance, your straight spine. Even when you were a baby in your diaper sitting on the floor in front of the TV, we would laugh at your straight little back and your concentration.” They both laugh and it breaks the tension surrounding their task.

Descriptive scenes and memory flashes follow as mother and son piece together Richard's violent death with some of the surrounding witness statements.

The phone rings and Mark is first to pick up the receiver. He turns to look at his mother over his shoulder as he says, "Hi, Lance. How are you?" Christina shakes her head vigorously in response to his words and glance. He continues: "No, sorry. Mom is not here right now, but I will get her to call you back. Oh! Yes, the Key Largo meeting went well but we are more confused now than before. It looks like my father's death was more than just an accident. Oh, yes, sorry you are still at the stage of what we were first told - a heart attack! Well, since then it became evident there had been a collision. Yes, all very strange. Anyway, I will let Mom fill you in when she gets back. Okay, bye." As Mark replaces the receiver he looks at Christina. "Mom, you are going to have to speak to him at some point. You can't just leave the poor guy hanging."

She replies quickly, "I know. I will. I don't want him involved in this drama. He'll also be an added distraction for me. We are going to have to stay focused. Okay, let's finish these last points, and then I will call the Key Largo Marine Patrol chief for an appointment. What was our last point?"

Mark nods in agreement as he reads from the computer screen: "...confirmation that the one-million-dollar life insurance policy was paid out to Monika with Investigator Hogan's assistance. He obtained the official death certificate and other necessary documents for her."

Christina adds, "September third. Your father's brother and estate representative, your uncle Andrew refuses to petition the Fischer will, believing it to be forged. Setting the wheels in motion, after which we file the only other will we have, which is the one that was mailed to Uncle Andrew, the one we call the anonymous will. Although we don't have an original and our fear is that the real one may already have been destroyed. The will's origins remain suspicious, but both Andrew and our handwriting analyst feel that it does represent the correct businesslike legal document Richard would have produced and the content is more appropriate to his wishes and intent, especially because it includes Richard's mother. At the time he presumable signed Monika's fake will, he was supporting his mother in a nursing home in Canada, and would never have excluded provisions for her or her continued healthcare. We'll still bring in FBI forensics to test the authenticity of both wills. Let the litigation begin! Oh, make a note that the only thing still outstanding from the Marine Patrol report is the toxicology report." Christina looks at Mark's back with a smile. He is waiting patiently to type the next words. "Okay. That's it."

He turns to face her after hitting the print button on the computer. The printer's whirring noise overshadows her next words as it spews out pages. "I can't help feeling some guilt that the telephone voicemails that I shared with Monika may have set this in motion."

Mark looks at her quizzically. "Mom, you know this would have happened anyway and probably in the works from the minute Monika left her husband to marry Dad. John, from Dad's office, said her ex-husband has already moved back in with her. Her real worry was always that you and Dad might end up back together again, and ruin her plans completely. Otherwise why call you out of the blue and tell you to stop calling yourself Mrs. St. John?"

Christina grins broadly. “Yes, that was really strange! Well, at least I had the satisfaction of exposing the truth to Richard before he died. She was so demanding. What audacity! Telling me to stop calling myself Mrs. St. John because she is *the* Mrs. St John now! My voicemail back to her gave me a great deal of satisfaction. I said that she would never be able to keep your father from seeing you. I said that every morning when Richard left for work, she would not (like many other wives) be wondering which women Richard was seeing that day, but whether or not he was with his own son!”

They are both smiling and Mark says, “Didn’t you also say that she was from the wrong side of the tracks or she would understand what protocol is? She just didn’t get it. You are a divorced mother and it is more than appropriate to keep the father’s name for the child’s sake.”

Christina laughs, throwing her head back. “Yes, I did say that, didn’t I? Then she ran telling tales to your father, stupid fool, because it just opened the door for him to call me and I could expose her true intentions. The last thing she ever wanted was for him to like me, or see me again.”

Mark grins happily and urges his mother to recount the retribution-type story again. “What did Dad say?”

“When he called to ask why I had left her such a nasty voicemail, I asked him how he could be so stupid and not realize what she was doing. It was clear Monika was trying to destroy his chance for any type of father-son relationship. I told him I was flabbergasted he couldn’t see what she was trying to do for her own financial gain. She thought by getting rid of you, as the rightful heir to his estate – it would become all hers. She was already wishing him dead! Richard said that if he felt this were the case he would be right out the door and assured me that you and his mother would inherit his estate. I could hear Monika ranting and raving in the background as she reacted to parts of our conversation. Now that I think about it, when she heard this last part, her noise in the background suddenly stopped. It’s possible she finally heard who was going to inherit your father’s estate, from his own mouth! I am sure your father was trying to appease her by making the call to confront me, but I can’t help feeling some guilt that perhaps our telephone conversation could have motivated her to plan his so-called accident!”

Mark's next remark makes Christina stiffen her back and elongate her neck, the body language of preparation. "You can't blame yourself Mom. Monika's greed was clear from the first day she met Dad. Everyone saw right through her, except Dad of course! It's interesting that she never anticipated how protective we would be of his memory. I suppose 'blood really is thicker than water'. She has no idea who she is dealing with, Mom. She thinks she is a tough bitch and that you are a pushover!"

Mark stands up quickly in response to papers being blown off the desk by a gust of wind. He strides across the room and shuts the open window. As he closes it he says, "Here comes the afternoon storm.... this time of day really reminds me of the thunderstorms in Africa. I still enjoy the noise of thunder and heavy rain hitting our roof."

Mark bends to pick up the papers off the floor. There is a new stillness in the room. Gathering them up into a pile, he stares at the one on top in disbelief. "Mom, did you see this? The fax date on this child support agreement between you and Dad? He couldn't have been in Miami signing Monika's so-called will. This fax puts him out of town on the same day the will is dated."

Christina jumps to her feet and moves over to Mark. Looking over his arm at the fax she says, "I do remember that now. He was out of town and our attorney had to fax him the final modification of your child support. Good grief! This could be further proof Monika's will was forged. We need to get your father's files as soon as possible to back-up his travel dates. He was always very meticulous with record keeping. His credit card receipts could be exactly what we need. Without proof, you know that her attorney will only twist things around. He could even claim that we falsified the fax date. It really is amazing how that gust of wind may actually change the course of your case. That was no coincidence. That page was blown right into your hands. You were meant to find that. There are no coincidences in life."

The wildlife oil painting on the wall by artist Brian Scott Dawkins was a symbolic gift for Christina as they left South Africa for that final trip to Florida to be with Richard. It now hangs on her living room wall as a reminder of the past and present. She made Mark promise it would never be sold, but

remain in the family as a stark reminder of their history and future.

The painting is exquisite in its life-like rendition. A pale blue sky covers distant green tree tops, with the yellow grasses of an African Savannah in the foreground. A lioness and her male cub are the focal point standing next to a dead tree. She is looking ahead at the oasis and clear blue sky. Her cub to her right side is taking one last look back at the dusty grasses.

Sadly, Christina remembered just how excited her ten-year-old son was when Richard called him from Miami and said that he wanted nothing else in his lifetime - other than to have his family together in the USA. That journey from South Africa would be one filled with anticipation and disappointment.

However, Christina and Mark had little doubt their destiny was exactly where it was intended to be, in the United States - as a family with or without Richard new freedom…

Chapter SEVEN

A Key Largo bar is noisily busy with the late afternoon spillover lunch crowd and a windy day. Christina, Mark and Lance are sharing a high top with an air of expectancy. Lance is seated between Mark and Christina, beer in hand. Christina has a wine glass on the table and Mark has a half-eaten sandwich on a plate in front of him. Lance is chatting; it is clear he is keeping their conversation light with occasional jokes leading to laughter.

The group's mood shifts to one of seriousness as Mark glances at his watch and says, "Well, it's nearly time. I'm surprised Chip Hogan agreed to meet us after we went to his captain and complained that the investigation was going nowhere. Hogan suddenly got the State Attorney's office involved. Didn't he say that one of the prosecutors may be coming with him today?"

Christina replies, "Yes. I'm surprised, too. I can't help feeling bad about going over his head to his captain, especially after I learned that Chip is near his retirement.

Obviously they were more concerned that we are questioning their 'final' report!" Mark chimes in, "He did nothing more, Mom, after our meeting. You can't feel bad. You and I know that he screwed up the investigation and let all the evidence go. He's the one who believed the BS about the wave-runners disappearing on the side of the highway. He only bothered to contact Mike, one of Dad's business partners from that long list of contacts we gave him. All the others tell us he never called. He called Mike only because you insisted and, of course, Mike verified our fears and told Hogan he also believed Dad may have been murdered. In fact, Mike said Hogan was the one trying to convince him otherwise, bringing up the ex-wife profiling and civil suit excuses again!"

Lance interjects, "I have no doubt the two of you have well and truly ruffled feathers down here. Expect them to be hostile toward you from now on. They band together, you know. This is the 'Boys Club' of Florida, and if you throw a few divorced men in the mix … well! Besides which, they think you are just fighting over money. In true Keys style, they will regard you as a threat to Investigator Hogan's future retirement."

Christina looks at him. "Yes, you are right. They were very hostile when I went to see them. I suppose it must appear strange that the divorced wife and son are trying to uncover the truth around Richard's death. Mark's Uncle Andrew is also going to be seeing them. In fact, he has already approached the Inspector General to have the investigation re-classified as a criminal case. We are meeting with him at his hotel on the way back, if that's okay. Need to update him. Monika is very convincing, you know. I am told she plays the seductive, helpless little girl very well."

Lance twists his mouth, nodding, "Oh, well, that will certainly work here. You did say this Hogan guy was divorced? I'll bet the department is worrying about a possible lawsuit from you, so they will be sure to squash anything as fast as possible."

Both Mark and Christina speak simultaneously. "Of course, we didn't think of that one." Mark continues, "I'm sure they don't realize, or care that we are fighting for the truth!"

Christina turns to Lance. "Thanks for coming with us. We really needed the moral support and to show some strength. The Miami group is banding together to cash-in with Monika."

Lance grins happily. He reaches under the table to squeeze Christina's knee, just as the uniformed Chip Hogan appears in the doorway with a tall, dark-suited, dark-haired man beside him. Hogan scans the room from his position and seeing Christina motions to her to come over. The three at the table look surprised. Christina and Mark get up saying, "Excuse us, Lance, they might want to speak with us alone."

Mark and Christina stride confidently toward Hogan and his companion while both men watch their approach. The handshakes are polite as mother and son are introduced to the state prosecutor and Hogan who then announces, "We have the toxicology report. I am sorry to have to tell you this, but Richard had marijuana in his bloodstream. The reality that it was an accident is now stronger than ever. This will mean closing the investigation."

Christina's shocked look says it all as she blurts out, "How could he have been so stupid. Stupid fool! Bloody stupid fool! But surely that does not mean his indiscretion must have caused his death. He did smoke occasionally, but not a lot. Sometimes he just made bad choices. It could still have been a homicide. We are working on evidence that the will his new wife produced could be forged. If we get this evidence would you consider investigating?"

Mark is standing speechless, his shoulders sinking in the hurt of the moment. Hogan continues, "For now, I am afraid this explains it all, as far as the department is concerned. I'm sorry. I wish you both well with your civil suit. If you can prove the forgery we may take another look. But, as you know the forgery may only mean she wanted to win the civil suit and not necessarily a motive for murder." Then, as quickly as the two men arrived, they leave.

Christina and Mark walk slowly back to join Lance who is watching them intently. His worried look is full of compassion for the disappointment that mother and son are displaying. "That was fast. Are you okay?" Christina replies slowly and with anger in her voice.

"Stupid fool! Believe it or not, he smoked a joint before getting on the wave-runner. Now they are trying to cite that as the whole reason for the accident and close the damn case! I always thought he would have been smarter than that!"

Mark's pain is etched into his young face as he says, "Now we know why Monika preferred to stay in the beach bar and not go out with them on the wave-runners. Remember, Mike said they had a little party earlier? That could have meant a discreet joint. After all, Monika was a known cokehead and a joint would have been a mild addition."

Christina is finding it hard to control her anger. "Careless damn fool - a joint! I can feel this one in my gut. Everybody knew he liked the occasional recreational drug. That was one of the reasons I left him. Between the damn bars, drugs and womanizing, I just couldn't deal with it anymore. But, I'd love to know who fired up the joint. I can't help thinking that this stinking joint may have been part of their plan."

Lance is cringing in reaction to Christina's outburst. He reaches into his pocket for his wallet and with his other hand reaches for his keys on the table. "Hey, let's pay and get outa here. Where are we headed for the meeting with Andrew?"

Mark and Christina do not need prompting. They are pale with the shock and disappointment of the moment. Their body posture and glistening eyes are evidence of their racing thoughts. Christina's reply comes as she walks briskly to the car. "Andrew's hotel is just off the highway in North Miami." Lance climbs into the driver's seat. "I'll wait in the car or drive around while you meet him, if that's okay? Not sure if I'm ready to meet Uncle Andrew just yet." Christina agrees with a sigh of relief.

The highway ride is painfully silent. Christina and Mark gaze pensively out of their side windows. Lance stares at the road ahead. He is not sure what the mood is, so chooses to remain silent.

The lifeless rhino and her baby are both lying on their right side, legs rigid in the air. Their torsos are swollen. The blood around the mother's face and blood-soaked ground bear evidence to the cause of her death. Her missing horn, hacked and sawn off her body making her look more like a hippo and less like the proud rhino she was.

Mark's tears streamed down his eight-year old cheeks. He wiped his nose with the back of his shirtsleeve. Christina was trying to console her son. His question was simple. "Why?"

Christina's heart was heavy that her child had to bear witness to such a harsh lesson in life - man's greed based on unfounded superstition and callous killing. A rhino horn would fetch a good price in the Far East where the grounded horn powder is a prized aphrodisiac. She tried to apologize for mankind and to explain the scenario to Mark.

"I am so sorry you had to see this Mark. It is insanity that anyone would kill these beautiful creatures for money, or believe that a rhino horn would help anyone get better at anything if you eat it the powder! It is a pity that the game rangers couldn't catch these poachers beforehand. This is why they have to carry guns too, not only to protect the tourists on the conservation farm from any wildlife attack, but also to protect the wonderful wildlife. This is part of what we are trying to do on the conservation farm, protect and preserve these wonderful creatures. There are only very few rhinos left in the world now."

Mark's words, uttered between his heart-retching sobs, surprised Christina in their spiritual nature and his young age.

"Soon there will be nothing left for them to kill. What then Mommy? Will God ever forgive them? Didn't he ask us to love one another and to protect his animals?"

from an earthly goal…

Chapter EIGHT

Mark's firm knock on the North Miami hotel door is expected. It is opened almost immediately aided by a gust of wind. Andrew's frame fills the doorway and they are greeted with hugs and a quick question. "Windy day, eh! Well, what did our friends at the Marine Patrol have to say?"

Christina's shaking head and grimace seem to say it all as she greets Andrew and a fair-haired woman in her fifties seated on the bed. "Hello, Karen," she says, and Mark echoes, "Hello, Aunty Karen."

Andrew looks worried. "Didn't go well, eh?" Andrew's habitual interjection is a giveaway of his Canadian roots; he is best described as an older version of Mark in body type and mannerisms. There is little doubt they are related.

Christina responds. "Well, this one was a sidewinder! I hate to tell you this Andrew, but I am afraid your brother made a bad choice. He was stupid enough to smoke a joint before he got on the wave-runner!"

Andrew shakes his head in disbelief. “Well that’s blown it out of the water now, I suppose. What are they going to do?”

Mark’s reply says it all. “Absolutely nothing!” Andrew motions for them to sit down. Mark slumps into the armchair while Christina sits near Karen. Andrew’s face is etched with deep disappointment. He sighs deeply as he moves to the corner fridge and opens the door, exposing three shelves lined with beer bottles. Christina’s glance into the fridge is followed by her discreet smile, which is picked up by Mark; they exchange a knowing look. Andrew offers them a drink, reaching into the fridge to grab a bottle. They decline as he flops on the edge of the bed. His large shoulders are slumped in disappointment. He takes a gulp of the beer and immediately exhales with a long, slow breath.

Andrew takes another sip before saying, “Yep, we St. Johns always like a party. Pity Richard didn’t resist it this time. Still, you’d think the obvious motive of a forged will and the suspicious circumstances of his death would be enough for them to continue. Why can’t we insist on a polygraph for Kenny and the whole damn lot?”

Karen stands, revealing some difficulty of movement and shifts to the window to look thoughtfully at the afternoon sun beginning to set. Christina watches, saying, “Different laws here, Andrew. Polygraphs just don’t stand up in our courts. In fact, not much does. It all depends on how good your attorney is and, of course, attorneys are evaluated on how expensive they are. You can literally get away with murder if you can afford the best attorney.”

Andrew looks a little confused and almost disbelieving at Christina’s last statement. He notices Christina’s eyes on his wife and comments proudly, “Isn’t she doing well? Since the stroke she has come back by leaps and bounds.” Karen regards him lovingly, saying, “Thanks to my husband. He has taken such good care of me. Not many husbands would be caught changing their wife’s diaper. Or have been so patient.”

Christina nods. “You are lucky to have each other.”

Andrew shifts to the role of taking charge. “We’d better plan our next move. I am sure they are scheming as we speak. You never know, they could have engineered the pot party at exactly the right moment in time.”

Mark takes the hotel notepad and pen off the desk. "I'll make notes. Maybe a few bullet points of the events so far would help us decide the next move." Andrew looks at him with pride, "Good boy! A true St. John."

Karen looks back at them from the window. "You know, Monika has made no offer of any of Richard's personal belongings or photographs to a family member. When Andrew and I were at Richard's house after the funeral, I asked for a photograph on the table of the three of us on the boat - Richard, Andrew and myself - and she just ignored me. I still can't believe how happy she looked after the funeral. She is really creepy. She scares me."

Andrew looks at Christina and Mark, reinforcing his wife's comment with, "Yes, can you believe that - not even a photograph! You know what Mark, I have one of Richard's at home and I'll send it to you when we get back to Canada." Mark's face lights up as he smiles appreciatively. "Thanks, Uncle Andrew. Anne Carter gave me a pen with Dad's name engraved on it. He left it at their farm after signing some documents with them."

Andrew stands and takes Karen's arm, leading her back to the bed where he seats her with a pillow at her back. "That was nice of Anne. How are they doing, by the way? Good thing she passed that newspaper cutting to you at the funeral, or we may still believe the 'died of a heart attack' bit from Monika. "

Christina shifts a little to allow Karen more room and replies, "They're doing well. They are a classic cattle-ranching couple. He still rides the range at nearly 75 and she is truly the matriarch of the family. I usually stop in Kissimmee to see them on my way back from Home Shopping headquarters in St. Pete - I'm marketing my new line of cosmetics through HSN, so I get to see them pretty often. She really does miss Richard. They were close and probably the only ones around him who were genuine friends to him. Having lost her own parents and two of her children, she understands death well. More importantly, she understood how important it would be for Mark to have some tangible items to hold on to in memory of his father. She is convinced Richard was murdered."

"I'm ready," Mark interjects, pen in hand. Christina smiles and, looking thoughtful, starts the chronicle of events.

"I suppose it is best to start with the wills. So, the Fischer will, as we call it, is the one produced by Monika Fischer St. John and filed with the courts for probate. As you have said, Andrew, it left everything to Monika, which is inconceivable."

Andrew replies, "Yes, it's absolute rubbish. Richard would never have left his entire estate to any one woman. He would also never have cut out his son, nor the whole St. John family and especially his own mother. I don't believe the signature on this will is my brother's. They tried to engineer it to look and sound more authentic by naming me as second personal representative, not expecting to get stuck with me. They certainly didn't expect their friend Alain to have a conscience and withdraw as the first named Personal Representative of the estate. Next, I unexpectedly received that second will in the mail from an anonymous friend. It looks more like something Richard would have written, but there is no way of proving it unless we find the original."

Mark looks up from his writing. "The original and true will may have been destroyed if they found it first. They needed to get their fake will into the probate system first…"

Christina continues. "In early October, I met with Metro Dade Police to discuss the existence of two wills. They say they will investigate, but that they have only eighteen investigators for the entire county, and we would not get priority. Far worse crimes are going on, according to them. Then it gets classified as a civil suit and they back off after Monika and her crowd muddied the waters by using me as their example of the divorced-wife-type profiling. Many of these men are divorced and may have their own relatable personal issues. Andrew, in the interim you found an attorney in Miami via the Yellow Pages?"

Andrew looks up with confidence. "Yes, and they are a large, respectable firm."

Christina frowns. "Andrew, you need to watch them. You know, when we first arrived in Florida, Richard gave us all the same advice. He didn't trust any of them. He told us never to own anything substantial like property because then your worth becomes the motive for a lawsuit. His word for them was 'bloodsuckers.' He eventually hired an in-house attorney to handle all his legal stuff. At the time I really thought he was overreacting and becoming paranoid. That is, until I learned from my own experiences. I am not saying that they are *all* bad. I have worked with a few that I trust and who became attorneys for all the right reasons, but many see it purely as a business."

Andrew frowns. "I don't know about that. This is a big firm and I think they will do a good job. They have assured me they will guide me through this."

Christina is shaking her head. "Oh, I am sure they will. Haven't they already advised you to bring Richard's money back from Zurich? Now, Andrew, you do realize that is the end of the money? The attorneys will find any excuse to bill the hell out of the estate and take it all! Richard moved the money away for a reason - to stop attorneys from laying their hands on it. He was in a couple of business disputes. He knew that attorneys usually back off and settle if they know they will not be paid, or if there is nothing more available to take. Haven't they also managed to sell Richard's Gulfstream Jets, Ferrari, and boats pretty quickly? Considering what they sold all of this for, it was probably to their own friends in the first place. This was also a smart way to keep their cash flow liquid, not for the beneficiaries, but for the attorneys' constant monthly legal bills!"

Andrew becomes agitated; reacting to his decisions being questioned. "I can't believe they are allowed to do that."

Christina notices his agitation. "Don't say I didn't warn you. This system is very, very different from Canadian law. Remember, here they take their fees first and monthly - out of the available estate cash even before the IRS or any other creditors. I was informed by our attorney that according to Florida estate legislation, the named children or other beneficiaries rank about tenth on the list to benefit. Then, if you complain about an attorney's billing practices to the Florida Bar, they will tell you that the attorney has to agree to the complaint before it can be filed. Every country is somewhat different. You are used to Canadian law, where you can file your complaint against an attorney with the courts and it will be heard. The attorney will then have to lower or correct any unethical billing."

Andrew roars with laughter. "Oh, that is ridiculous, Christina. I can't believe the legal system here is that strange. This sounds absurd!" She looks at him with surprise and is about to respond when Mark signals her discreetly with his eyes not to do so.

Christina ratchets it down. “Well, we will just have to wait and see. The last thing I will say on this is that USA politicians are mostly made up of attorneys, or former attorneys who pass laws to protect themselves. There is not much you can do to change the system. This is not just my opinion, our friends, the Beaumont’s had their estate almost wiped out by attorneys when her own father died, and that was almost 50 years ago.”

Christina does not miss a beat as she continues, “Her grandfather was a governor who had a county named after him. Even with that political clout she still could not change the process. She is always warning us to avoid long-term legal battles. Worldwide, the legal system has changed. It is no longer the honorable profession it was. The attorneys blame feuding families and drawn-out divorces as an excuse to keep churning ridiculous bills each month until the estate has dwindled - until they can’t take anymore. She said lawyers actually believe the estate money IS theirs from the moment they sign the client.”

Mark is looking at them with concern. He recognizes the escalating hostility and changes its direction by interrupting their conversation with a question, “Uncle Andrew, what about Dad’s office files? They were all there when I went to the office the morning after the accident. Monika could not wait to get me out of there so she could get her hands on it all. The final lists of office and home contents that you received from Monika and her attorney are nowhere near the truth. He was a meticulous businessman and had everything filed. There is a great deal missing and in confusion. They had too much time between his death and your taking control as the estate personal representative. I am pretty sure they have already divvied up lots of his stuff to buddies and staff. Didn't Monika give my so-called sister the Bentley at the funeral to get rid of her? And what about the contents of Richard's safe and so on?"

Andrew says, "Yes, of course, Richard's partners and Monika are all blaming each other. We were too late in seizing the estate, but it really was because of the change in estate personal representatives. Only after I was officially appointed could I step in. Yes, I heard the same thing about the Bentley. It looks like Samantha took the car and left. Seems like all she really cared about was leaving with a big piece of the estate as quickly as possible."

Christina muses, "We first met Samantha at Disney World with Richard a few years ago. We were willing to accept that she might be his illegitimate daughter, but we really were deeply concerned at some of her comments. She was worried that Richard was going to marry Monika leaving his wealth to be split five ways! Not something you should be saying just as you meet your biological father's real family!"

Karen looks a little self-conscious as she says, "We thought we were helping by finding her for Richard. I was working at the hospital and managed to track down a birth certificate. It didn't have his name on it, but did have the name of the ex-girlfriend who claimed he was the father. Richard was missing Mark so much when you both left Toronto. We thought we were doing the right thing by tracking her down."

Christina switches the topic to the note-taking. "Okay, where were we? Yes, Richard's files and belongings. It's going to be hard to form a trail of his companies, investments and assets if the files are gone. I am sure the attorneys put her up to it and are hiding them somewhere to go through at their leisure before handing them over. The more the attorneys can muddle things, the longer it will take. And their hourly billing will just keep rolling on."

"Mom, I think Monika is in full control of all of this and that she has the important files in her possession. She is going through them with a fine-toothed comb. She believes Dad had a lot more money than seems apparent now. He was proud of his success and bragged about it to everyone. Sometimes his larger-than-life bragging made people think he was a billionaire – Monika thought so, too! Anyway, let's go over these points now." They turn to listen to Mark's notes.

"In July, very soon after Dad's death, the Fischer will, Monika's will, was the first one that came to light and was placed into probate by her attorney. In this will, she is named as sole beneficiary. You, Uncle Andrew, are named as second Personal Representative, probably to give the will an authentic tone. Further, Alain du Pont, a business acquaintance is named first Personal Representative who resigned shortly after that. We are forced to hire an attorney and Mom becomes the first objector as my guardian. Our doubts about the will are based on its contents and suspicious signatures. In August, Uncle Andrew receives a different will from an anonymous source, and he forwards it to Mom and me. This will has the same date as the Fischer one and is postmarked via Dad's office in Fort Lauderdale. It names my illegitimate sister, my Gran and me as beneficiaries. Uncle Andrew, you are named as sole Personal Representative. We then hire a document examiner to look at both wills. He maintains that both could be fraudulent. This is just one more reason to keep searching Dad's papers - there may be an even earlier will that could prove to be genuine."

Mark continues. "Then Mom and I file an official complaint of possible forgery on both wills with the Metro Dade Police. You, Uncle Andrew, meet with them to back up our complaint. As mentioned, they can't keep up with all their cases, but make an attempt at an investigation by speaking to a witness and to the attorney who it is now believed may have helped forge Monika's will. Their reluctance to pursue the investigation is based on the fact that it is now a civil case and they do not have the manpower to deal with grand theft. In the meantime, I have a birthday coming up and will turn 18. As a result, I will become the official objector…." Mark looks at Christina before making his final comment. “I’ll never forget how she tried to have you removed from that first hearing, Mom, because you were representing me. She was predictably ignorant of the law and the judge had to let her know that until I was eighteen, you had to be there.”

Christina smiles and responds with, “Yes, I’ll never forget the way she looked or the way she behaved at that hearing. My first face-to-face with her, and it had to be in court! I mean, really! Every time she didn’t get her way or just needed attention, she would bang her armload of bangles on the court’s table. She has obviously had some plastic surgery since then too, and probably where her life insurance money is going. The lines on her face are disappearing and the lips are suddenly swollen.”

Andrew laughs. He adds to the new conversation with, “That first hearing was classic. The tiny new gold-digger wife dressed like a slut sneering at the tall ex-wife in an up-do and a business suit. The judge has got to see through all of this!”

Everyone laughs and Christina adds, “The saddest thing was how cold she was. She was completely focused on the will and the cash. She should have at least pretended to be grieving.”

Andrew chips in with, "I am sure the judge summed up all of that pretty fast!"

Andrew's statement seems to reassure Mark, who nods and puts pen to paper again. "Okay, where were we? The objection is amended to indicate that we believe the Fischer will is forged and the signature is not my father's. As well as new evidence we found with a date on a faxed document. Then you also confirmed that Dad might actually have been in Canada on the date the will was supposed to have been signed by him in Florida. We can only prove this once we have the files from his office and can create the paper trail of his travels. Are you sure this was about the same time as Carol's 21st birthday party in Canada, and Dad was there?"

"Absolutely sure. Carol was your father's godchild and he was definitely at her twenty-first birthday celebration. Monika did not come with him. She wasn't interested in creating bonds with us. They think they were smart in forging a will. But they may have chosen the wrong date for him to have signed it!"

Mark shifts in his seat to lean on the other armrest as he continues, "Okay, here we go. Now, let's compare the statements of the accident witnesses. Kenny said they were cruising toward a marina. He was to port and Dad to starboard, traveling in a northeasterly direction. He said that the two vessels impacted, ejecting both of them. Now Kenny said all three of them, including Avi, were there when the collision happened, but Avi's report said he left them alone for about fifteen minutes and was not there. Who the hell are we supposed to believe? I really can't believe these contradictory witness statements were taken by Marine Patrol and they did not think it was suspicious!"

Mark looks up. "Uncle Andrew, you met with the Marine Patrol and got the same results?" There is anger in Andrew's reply. "Yes, a formal investigation into my brother's death may be denied."

Andrew's face is puffed and red. He moves to the fridge and takes out another bottle and gestures it to the others. Christina responds, "No, thanks, Andrew, we have a long drive home. Then let's not forget what Richard told Mark on the phone a few days before the Key Largo trip. He said he did not really want to go to Key Largo, but instead was hoping to go to his farm in Ocala for the weekend. He was looking forward to a permanent move to the farm next year. Apparently Monika did not want to move to the farm at all; she wanted to stay with her friends in Miami. I am sure this, plus the fact they were fighting constantly about money, led to the Key Largo incident. The trip was a reconciliation she suggested after their brief separation. This may all have been pre planned."

Karen comforts her husband with a hand on his thigh. He responds by placing his hand warmly over hers as he continues, "I just can't believe this has happened. I never liked her from the minute I met her. I don't know what he saw in her. He said she had something to do with the wealthy Bear furniture family, but then that turned out to be BS. She arrived to meet us in her trendy, Miami-type jeans and black leather jacket look. You know, Richard was always trying to act younger and to fit in with the trendy set. Look where it landed him! Christina, you will find this funny. You know our Mom really loved you. Towards the end, when she was in the nursing home, Richard would visit and in the beginning Monika would come along, too. Mom started pretending to be senile every now and again and called her Christina! She really didn't like Monika and never forgave Richard for not working harder to get you back. Mom had all her faculties till the day she died."

Christina smiles and says, "Yes, I think we heard that story before. There is absolutely no way he'd have excluded your Mom from his will. That was a bad mistake on their part when they put that will together. From what I hear, Monika's an extremely good manipulator. You know, Richard always said, "Who motivates the motivator?" And in this case, who manipulates the…?" She stops mid-sentence, not wanting to say anything derogatory about Richard within the family group.

She continues, "Richard used to be proud of the fact he was a good businessman, as well as becoming Consul General of Liberia - an amazing story in itself."

Andrew smiles. "He was always the lucky brother. Yes, that was a helluva story. I mean, he finds a black guy who was mugged outside the Churchill Hotel in London and he helps him with some cash and Band-Aids. The guy turns out to be some sort of Liberian royal figure who then appoints Richard as his Consul General in Canada in gratitude. He always was at the right place at the right time."

Christina replies, "Yes, he always had a great sense of timing - just not this time!"

Mark responds, "Mom, you know Dad didn't question his own mortality any more than he questioned his trust in those around him to execute his true wishes." Andrew, Karen and Christina look at each other and smile at his wisdom.

Christina holds her palm up, looking at Mark. "I have no idea where that comes from. He had two crazy parents. He really is the stable one in the family. Mark doesn't deserve this, and Richard did not deserve to die like this."

Mark stands, putting the notes in his pocket and placing the pen back on the hotel desk. He looks at his mother and she follows his lead. "Andrew, Karen, we'd better start back. We have that hearing in the morning and then the deposition the next day. They are piling on the pressure to wear us down! Will you be there tomorrow, Andrew?"

"Yes, and immediately after the hearing I have meetings with my attorneys. There are a few things to go over with the estate. They are trying to force Monika to hand over Richard's documents and we need to get to your requisition for Mark's college fees. Oh, by the way Christina, how is your business going?" Andrew's last question is tinged with a little sarcasm, which does not go unnoticed by both mother and son.

Christina replies. "Not very well right now, Andrew - between trips to hearings, depositions and Marine Patrol. I am still trying to keep things together. You know all the traveling I have to do to Home Shopping in St. Petersburg for the TV shows, and then rush back to manufacture the cosmetics."

Mark adds, "The attorneys know what we're faced with and how the trips mess with my schoolwork, too. They are doing it intentionally, trying to force us to give up faster. We have no option but to travel to them in Miami. Of course, they are not traveling anywhere."

Andrew adds, "Me, I'm traveling also. I'm trying to arrange it so that I'll come down from Canada every month. It must be hard when your legal appointments are every week."

Mark adds, "Sometimes twice a week. But they don't realize how stubborn Mom is. Dad used to say she was the most pigheaded person he knew!" Everyone laughs as Christina and Mark move toward the door.

Andrew stands, placing his beer bottle on the side table and walks them to the door. “I just can’t understand the legal system here - the depositions part. It seems strange to give your opponent all your evidence before you go to court. Doesn’t that give them time to create lies to counteract it?”

“It was originally designed to reduce the overload of court cases and cut back on court time. But, you are quite right. It gives the bad guys time to come up with lies and forgeries to counteract everything. They can get pretty rough. Imagine sitting across a table from the woman you think murdered your father and not reacting when she taunts you. Mark has handled everything really well, and now he is going to have to face her again tomorrow. I think she believes he will be a pushover because of his age and good manners. She has no idea who she is dealing with.”

Mark beams with confidence and says, “Mom, we’d better get going. I still have some schoolwork to do.”

There are hugs all around as they leave the darkening room and Andrew makes a parting comment. “Okay, you two, you need to gear up for this fight. You need to be strong and continue to push for the full investigation into Richard's death. There is only so much I can do from Canada. I also can't compromise my position as the estate personal representative. I will see you in the morning!"

As Christina and Mark walk toward the lobby, Christina says heatedly, "He just does not get it."

Mark holds up his hands in despair. "You are not going to change his opinions, Mom. Uncle Andrew believes he is right. He is the epitome of a chauvinistic, older generational man - besides being a St John. Do you honestly think he believes we may have any more experience or knowledge than him? "

"Hold on," Christina says, dialing Lance from her cell phone to arrange their pickup. Following her brief call, she rolls her eyes before saying, "Andrew doesn't understand the legal system. The attorneys are going to take full advantage of his ignorance. He also gets paid from the estate as the representative, so it is money for him anyway."

Mark holds the hotel lobby door open for his mother. "I am sure he thinks he earned the money. Remember, Dad was moving them to Florida. Monika was really mad about that!"

"Yes, I know he means well and he wants justice for his brother, but as usual I am the single parent facing the possible loss of my business and trying to get through this lawsuit. He just keeps pushing me to investigate and pressure our attorney. This takes money - our money! I am the one getting deeper into debt. I still can't believe your uncle would not just agree to fund your college fees from the estate. He could, you know."

Outside, Mark leans against the wall and Christina half-seats herself on the corner of a planter. Dusk is casting long shadows around them. Mark continues. "Just imagine how Uncle Andrew must be feeling as a Gold Shield detective, proficient in polygraph who has worked homicide and there is absolutely nothing he can do for his brother! It is totally out of his control. You know how difficult that is for a St. John - lack of control?"

They spot the SUV driving up the street as Mark says, "I'm guessing the estate attorneys are advising Andrew not to pay my college fees. It would mean less money for them. Talk about greed! We are only asking for my first year's fees out of an estate worth a few million. Then we have Monika who believes it's all hers anyway!"

The SUV swerves gently towards them with Lance in the driver seat, as Mark continues. “Well, here’s Lance. It probably feels weird for him right now. You really are keeping him at arm’s length. What are you going to do?”

Christina confides in a whisper, “I really don’t want to hurt him, but inevitably there could be more hurt. He is a nice guy and deserves my honesty. I just feel no connection with him anymore. Your dad’s death has forced us all onto a completely different life path.”

There is a hippo pool between the thatched restaurant building and Yaya's home (Mark's grandmother) so the timing of closing the restaurant and going home had to be carefully planned... the pathway ran right along the edge of the hippo pool. Seven year old Mark is walking ahead of his mother on the path going home and it is shortly before dusk. The hippos are watching the pair with just their snouts, ears and eyes exposed above the water. There is the occasional snort from them too.

Mark asks, " Yaya said it is never wise to come between the hippo and its pool - especially at dusk when they leave the pool to walk and feed. What happens when you cross the hippo's path - like that mother and baby over there in the pool?"

Christina responds. " Choose the wrong path and come between the hippo and its water, or more especially between the mother and her baby - and she will kill. There are more people killed in Africa by hippos than any other animal."

Mark picks up his pace a little. "She is only protecting her baby just like you always do mom and we will just stick to our path."

warm tears shed…

Chapter NINE

The judge is leaning his large frame to the side in his chair. He is conveying a sense of forced tolerance. In front of him a long red oak table forms a T-angle to his desk; thus the attorneys and clients seated on either side all face him. His black robe and seated position at the table represent his authority in the windowless Miami Court chambers. On one side of the table, Mark and Christina are seated alongside a small, round, balding and bespectacled man - their attorney, Sergio. Across the table is a lanky, sharp-featured, red-headed man who introduces himself as Kurt Dubb, attorney for Monika Fischer. Next to him another attorney sits down and announces himself as Gary, attorney for the estate curators. Gary's dark suit is stretched over his large, overweight frame. Sweat beads trickle down his brow to the top of his dark-rimmed glasses. He wipes them away with the back of a chubby hand, as the other hand places a pile of documents on the table. He glances around the table and acknowledges those already seated with a brief nod.

Andrew St. John enters the room and apologizes for his tardiness, explaining that the drive to downtown Miami was fraught with traffic problems. Kurt nods and adds, "The same reason my client is running late, Judge." The judge looks at him and gazes at the group saying, "Here we are again, the St. John litigation. Well, I don't think it is a saint-like litigation at all. I cannot believe we are here because of college fees and that you will not let this child go to college."

He points at Mark. "Why hasn't the estate curator at least offered him a loan until the case is settled? I understand I can't technically award these college fees, but something needs to be done here."

Kurt jumps at the opportunity to say, "That's exactly what I want to suggest, Your Honor. A loan from the estate. That way Mark can go to school now." His last few words are overshadowed by the opening door and the entrance of a petite figure. Monika is dressed in a brown spandex slack suit with a short peplum-style jacket. The tight, thin spandex fails to hide some cellulite on her thighs. A noisy row of bangles shifts up and down her arm as she sits down next to her attorney. Her swollen lips bear evidence of new collagen treatments. She stares angrily across the table at Christina and Mark, giving her bangles a shake for attention. She glances up and down at Christina's elegant pink business outfit with disdain.

Christina and Mark do not acknowledge her entry, or her presence. Both are looking stoically at the judge. The judge notices Monika's last action. His eyes show his impatience. Looking across at Sergio, he asks, "Well, where are we with this will contest case? How much longer is it going to take?"

Sergio looks uncomfortable as he replies, "We are still in our discovery stage, Your Honor. We need more time to complete our discovery. This is not a cut-and-dry case. There are extenuating circumstances."

Monika's glee is shown by the immediate broad grin that proves to be an awkward, crooked pull on her plumped mouth. Her satisfaction is echoed by her attorney, who jumps in at the chance to show how reasonable they are trying to be. "Your Honor, I have been trying to wrap this up as fast as possible. We have suggested mediation and we are ready for that."

The judge looks at him with a direct stare, showing some annoyance at Monika's noisy bangles now repeatedly in contact with the table top. "Then perhaps you should mediate and see what happens. I am sorry I cannot award these fees, but I do feel the estate curators should offer this young man a loan in the meantime. If I awarded these college fees I would have to make awards to all the other creditors ahead of him and I do not believe the estate is quite ready for that yet. Is it?"

After this question he looks expectantly at Gary, who answers quickly: "That is correct, you're Honor. We are far from finished with this estate." Andrew is nodding in agreement beside him.

The judge corrects his leaning frame and abruptly sits upright in the armchair, his body language an indication that the hearing is complete and he has made a decision. "Well, then, mediate these college fees as a loan." He looks at Mark with a follow-up. "I am sorry, young man. I am not in a position to award these but I feel your father would have wanted you to go to college, so this is all I can do right now."

Monika looks elated that the loan means that she may not have to sacrifice any funds from what she regards as hers – the entire St. John estate. She looks directly at Mark across the table hoping he will see her ear-to-ear grin. Together with her attorney she thanks the judge, who scowls back at them. The judge stands up and the others in the room follow his lead.

Before leaving the judge's chambers, Monika blurts out another trilling, "Thank you, Your Honor." The judge is walking through the doorway, his back is to the group and he does not reply.

Mark avoids any eye contact with Monika, instead turning to Sergio and Christina with a brief shrug. Monika takes one last gleeful look at them over her shoulder before walking down the passage with her attorney in tow.

Sergio ushers Christina and Mark into an adjoining room. Andrew and Gary are left standing in the lobby area. Sergio says, "I asked Andrew and Gary to give us a few minutes before they join us to discuss the college loan."

The three huddle around the table in a bland and colorless anteroom to plan their next move. Christina opens the conversation with, "Interesting comment from the curators' attorney, hey? They are not finished with the estate yet! Of course not! There is still money left for them to take!"

Sergio looks at her over his rimless glasses as he replies with a heavy Cuban accent, "Yes, and you'd better believe that. Forgive me but I need to add, the estate attorneys *and* your Uncle Andrew, are raping the estate. The longer our litigation with Monika takes, the longer they have to take more. Both you and Monika may end up without a dime! The judge is right. You are going to have to settle with her at some point."

Christina and Mark are both indignant. Mark is first to reply. "Sergio! How can you even suggest we should settle with someone who we think murdered my father?"

Christina is next. "She will end up with nothing, which is just what Richard meant her to have. He was generous enough to give her a life insurance of a million and even something in the pre-nup. How dare she think she is entitled to his entire estate! Stupid coke-headed bitch! She was trained as a nail tech but never worked as one. When she met Richard she was a salesperson in a clothing store."

Mark looks at her knowingly and he tries to calm his mother's tirade, "That's probably *why* she wants it all. He is not around anymore to feed her habit and her newly acquired lavish lifestyle. Its okay, Mom. She will end up with nothing! Didn't Uncle Andrew say he would push for my college fees?"

Christina sighs deeply and looks at Sergio and then at Mark. "No. He said that his co-curator and the accountant felt you should just go to a local community college like his son did and that the estate should not pay for it. Richard not only wanted you to attend college, he even included this stipulation in our final child-support agreement. Pity we can't let the judge know about the forgery and possible murder now."

Sergio replies, "No, by law, that kind of evidence is kept strictly for the trial. Of course, because of that, Monika's attorney jumped at the chance to force a mediation date for the contested will today - and it worked. We may not have any option now."

Mark looks at them both. His large hands are resting on the table. He appears relaxed and at ease in his dark suit. "Well, I am not his son. I am Richard St. John's son and I am proud of it. He wanted me to go to a good college and even made his wishes known in their divorce papers. If we have to mediate, then so be it. If it doesn't work out then we will go to trial. Sergio, set a mediation date with her attorney."

Christina looks at him with great pride. "Well done, my boy. It is becoming evident that her attorney does not want to go to trial. He doesn't seem to feel his case is as strong anymore. He probably realizes Monika has lied to him and wants to block us from obtaining any further evidence by forcing us to settle via the mediation. Especially now, after he was in Sergio's offices and witnessed the document examiner's discoveries. It must have been a shock for him to know that your father's signature and initials on her will - were more than likely forged. I still have a tough time believing anyone could forge a will."

Sergio smiles knowingly and says, "I know you are surprised about the forged will. This type of thing happens all the time here. The fact of the matter is the judge is angry. Clearly he likes you, Mark and wants the will contest to end so you can carry on with your life. He was a juvenile court judge so he may lean toward a child's future. He can also see that the estate is being eaten up in legal fees. Anyway, let's make a decision. Are we going to get the curators in now and ask them for that loan? I am surprised that your Uncle Andrew did not just agree to it - that we had to go through this whole hearing."

Mark replies, "Then his attorney would not have had the chance to earn anything! Anyway, yes, let's get them in here and finalize. I have to get back to school and Mom has to travel from here all the way to Home Shopping on the other coast."

Christina nods. She is holding her neck. Mark notices, saying, "Is it another one of those headaches starting?" She nods again and pulls her mouth to the side in confirmation.

Sergio stands up. He opens the door and motions for the two men waiting outside to join them. Andrew and Gary take seats across from them at the table as Sergio begins. "We are ready to request the college funds as a loan with a repayment date following the close of the estate."

Gary smiles at him. "Andrew and I have discussed this and we agree. We will allow it as long as it is repaid."

Sergio adds with some sarcasm, "The way things are going with your legal fees, you probably need this money back to cover your exorbitant fees. How long is this estate probate going to take, Gary?"

Andrew looks uncomfortable and is fidgeting. Gary sounds confident: "Our fees are our fees. This estate has too many loose ends and of course the unfortunate disappearance of all Richard's office files for nearly seven months hasn't helped. It just prolongs it all. We have to wait till we get those before we can even try to estimate how long the estate will take. Our fee situation is only going to get worse. The taxes still have to be addressed as well. I think you need to consider settling this case soon. Maybe then the files will suddenly reappear."

Christina's reply is curt. "Oh, I am sure Monika and her attorney will give up the files once they have finished going through them. They are pretending they don't know where they are. Bearing in mind Richard may even have had some further assets overseas, I am sure she is trying to find everything that's in those files before you get them. Our intention is to prove she was directly involved in the conspiracy to kill Richard. I believe we are close to finding the last bits of evidence we need. The problem is some of this evidence may very well be in those files.

Our advantage is that she is unaware of what we are looking for, or she would remove that, too."

Sergio returns to his assumed role as the room's group leader and reminds them, "The judge has ordered mediation so we may have to agree. Obviously we will have to depose her first. I'll get a mediation date." He stands and leaves the room.

Now that a conclusion is reached, Andrew changes the conversation and says, "I think the judge sees right through all of this. He looked angry when he saw Monika's reaction to you not getting your college fees paid outright. He knows she is not the best stepmother in the world. She is showing her character. He saw her true colors today. This can only work in your favor."

Mark's reply is the final statement within the group as they all stand to leave the room. "I have never had a stepmother. Please refer to her as my father's wife."

The group files out of the room and splits up in the court hallway with handshakes. Christina and Mark enter the harsh light of the Miami afternoon and walk toward the parking garage. Christina looks up at her son. "We should grab a bite before hitting the road. It's a long drive."

Mark looks happy at the suggestion. “Good idea. Let’s go to the restaurant where I had lunch with Dad. Remember, the one on the Intracoastal. It’s not far from here.” Christina’s face shows a little reluctance as she agrees.

A fifteen-minute drive takes them to the busy, Intra-coastal waterway restaurant. The valet quickly helps Christina from the car at the same time waving at the car behind them. She turns to Mark. “Wow, it’s busy. Hope we can get a table. This feels a little weird. Your dad was waiting right here for you when I dropped you off for that lunch with him.”

As they walk into the trendy, shiny black and dull-chrome interior, she continues, “He was wearing the preferred Miami-black shirt and pants. He seemed smaller than I remembered, but then I had not seen him in just over a year. I remember how proud he looked as you walked up to him. You towered above him. I remember how he held up his hand over his head to acknowledge the fact. I drove away that day feeling your pain, wanting desperately for him to get beyond the Monika manipulation. I said a little prayer for both of you as I drove off.”

Mark is asking the pretty hostess for a table and hearing there is a twenty-minute wait. He turns to his mom and in a sad voice says, "Yes, I remember that day. Should we wait? Twenty minutes. It's not too bad. These Miami restaurants can be forty minutes most times."

Christina nods as the hostess ushers them to the bar area to wait for their table. Mark leans against the bar as he orders two lemonades from the bartender.

Christina hops up onto the bar stool seat next to him and continues her chatter. "You know, it seemed like an eternity before you called me to pick you up. I had been killing time by window-shopping and having numerous Cuban coffee shots. So I was buzzing. My heart sank when you came out alone. Then I saw you smiling. This was a good sign and my spirit lifted. But when you said that he had invited me in for a drink, my throat closed! I was very reluctant but your hopeful eyes said it all. I am really pleased I did come in and we spent that time together."

"Yep, I even remember what you were wearing - your jeans, boots and a suede jacket. Dad said you looked great!" They both laugh as she continues. "My legs felt numb as I walked in as nonchalantly as possible. Your dad was seated at the bar and as he looked up with a smile, he said 'Hi, babe!'"

Mark sees the tears welling up in her eyes and says, "I remember I was surprised at how civil you were with each other. Remember, we reminisced about some of our travels together. You even laughed about some of your battles. I think I must be the most traveled young person in the world. I mean, how many countries did we meet Dad in? I think I went to every country other than the Middle East, Russia and parts of Africa before I was 10 years old!" Again they both laugh. Mark is watching the pretty hostess walking past them as her eye catches his. Christina smiles, "She is cute. You really do have your father's genes."

Mark laughs and continues with the reminiscing. "Dad was so proud of his new deal. He said it was going to make him a billionaire. Interestingly, this is the only business Monika is after, the one involving naturally-based pesticides. It all starts making so much sense now. Remember how toward the end of that afternoon he became quite forlorn and then suddenly launched into some of his marital problems with Monika, saying his stepchildren were never grateful for anything he did for them and they did not even greet him in the mornings? He also said that he was continuously arguing with Monika about money. I was not sure how to react, I guess he needed someone outside his circle to talk to. I was kind of shocked it was us. He must have really felt stressed-out."

Christina is sipping her tall lemonade, looking over her glass at him. "Yes, that was so unexpected that I was not sure how to react to it. I know how difficult it was for your father to even begin to admit he may have made a mistake by marrying her or taking on the role of stepfather. I do remember very clearly that when you went to the bathroom, he thanked me for raising a fine young man. He was amazed at how you had managed to stay so stable and good through some very trying times between two hostile parents. He even admitted to the fact that I had been right in the past when I had called him a control freak. When you came back I made him repeat what he'd said about you."

Mark smiles broadly. "Yes, that was funny - and really nice. Thanks, Mom, and I suppose I should also say thanks, Dad. I am sure he is listening."

Christina shivers. "I just got a chill down my spine. I am sure he is here. I do remember whenever we spoke to him on the phone there was always one of Monika's kids screaming or crying in the background for attention. Hell, I would have put a stop to that! I am really surprised he did not."

Mark replies, but seems to be a little distracted by someone behind them. "The screamer was Monika's younger one. Absolute brat, he was always screaming… Mom, look over there, behind us. I think that's Michael sitting at that table. Crazy coincidence, but I am sure it is him."

Christina turns and reacts immediately by jumping off the bar stool. With Mark behind her, they approach the good-looking young black man who looks at them in surprise. He grins, showing perfect white teeth. He waves at them as they walk toward him.

Michael is the first to speak as he leans back in his chair. "My word, this kid looks more like Richard St. John all the time. Wow! Mark, you are looking good, man! You have even lost that St. John tummy roll - like your father had. This was his favorite restaurant, you know?" They laugh and Michael stands to hug them both.

Michael continues, "Monika made Richard run nearly five miles a day to lose that tummy roll of fat. I used to joke with him that he should not be doing it, with his high blood pressure and all! Would you like a glass of champagne, Mrs. St. J?"

Christina laughs, "No thanks, Michael. You know you never stopped calling me Mrs. St. J. Right from the first time I met you in the Seychelles, through your working life with us, and even through his marriage to Monika!"

Mark reacts to Michael's previous statement, saying, "Really, Mom, you should have seen it. Dad used to arrive back from those runs with his hair standing on end and all red in the face, while she looked fine. I think she was trying to kill him even then!" Michael raises an eyebrow and quickly changes the subject by complimenting Mark on his dapper-looking suit. Christina replies for him. "Mark has all the right genes from his father, including his excellent taste in clothes."

Mark beams. It is obvious they are all pleased to see each other. An attractive blond girl approaches them and

Michael quickly introduces them. “Jill, this is Richard St. John’s son, Mark, and his ex-wife, Christina. We all met in the Islands of the Seychelles when I was a teenager. ”

Jill smiles at Mark saying, “Hell, he looks just like him. Sorry for your loss - and nice to meet you, Christina.”

Christina acknowledges the girl’s statement: “He is a clone of his father. Nice to meet you too, Jill.”

The newcomer sits down at Michael’s table and Michael gestures an invitation to Mark and Christina to do the same.

They remain standing as Christina says, “Thank you, Michael, but we are waiting for our table. We are both starving and I am sure you can understand we had one of those awful legal hearings again today.”

Michael rolls his eyes in sympathy and replies, “I have heard a little about what you are going through. You know, I really miss that man. It was such a pity we ended up in that damn lawsuit, all because of Monika. Things ended pretty badly for me and Richard. That little thing managed to get rid of anyone around Richard who really cared about him.”

Christina looks at him, sadness etched into her face.

"Yes. I heard that, too. You had been friends from when you were a teenager. He really trusted you as his business partner. I am really sorry it ended so badly between the two of you. If you had still been around, perhaps things may have been very different for Richard."

Michael nods, his reply tinged with amazement as he says in his gentle, British-accented voice, "I just can't believe it. I introduced them, you know. I feel so bad about it now. While you were back in Africa packing up for your move to Florida, she came into the picture. I thought it would just be a fling and the two of you would still get back together. I mean, I know he had asked you to marry him again and you refused. That was wise. He told me you wanted to live together for a while, see how things went. Understandable, I suppose. You had a lot of water under the bridge. The next thing I knew he was going to marry her! It was so painfully clear she was only there for his money! She proceeded to get rid of all of us - all the old guard by starting friction between all of us. Damned shrewd, you know! Finally there was almost none of the old crowd left. She brought in her South Beach friends and her family. Talk about control! You would never expect it. She is such a little thing, although pretty feisty! I suppose that is part of the deception. I have actually been wondering if this was a plot between her and her previous husband, whom she divorced for Richard. They all remained good friends, which seemed very weird! I get upset even talking about it. Richard was naughty, too. When any of us tried to question his change of plans with you, he tried to convince us all to 'love to hate' you too. But I must tell you, part of the motivation was that she was a US citizen already and he was not. It was also painfully obvious that he really struggled with his new role as a stepfather to her two boys. He really disliked those kids. He kept saying they were spoiled brats who did not respect him and just wanted stuff all the time. I have absolutely no doubt Monika only married him for his money."

Christina replies with a quiver in her voice, "Yes, I'm sorry I did not agree to remarry him now. But I have to wonder if it would have changed anything with Monika. It could have been worse and probably another divorce for us! She got her hooks in and was not going to let go. Through the divorce blame game, we both tried desperately to live without each other. It was a situation that she took advantage of and played into."

The hostess approaches, menus in hand. She touches Mark's elbow and with a smile indicates the table is ready. Michael looks at Mark with deep sincerity in his eyes as he says, "Sorry we have to leave but we are meeting friends to watch the fireworks. Good luck, Mark. I know your father was and would still be, very proud of you. Take care of your mother, our one-and-only, Mrs. St. J."

As they walk away Christina comments, "He has aged well. There's only the slightest gray tinge to his peppercorn hair and he is still as charming as ever. He owes his success to your dad. They were good friends once upon a time. I hope we will see him again."

Christina and Mark are seated and order their meal from the waitress. Mark asks, "Mom, you have that glazed look of pain in your eyes again. Are you okay? I am really worried about your drive to St. Pete. I can take my schoolwork with me and drive you." Christina looks at him with gratitude, "Yes, you may have to do that, sweetie. The pain is getting worse. Hope it does not mean an ER visit. I have three on-air shows that I have to be bright-eyed and bushy-tailed for."

"Mom, you really need to see a specialist about those headaches."

"I know. I just don't have the time to deal with all of that right now. I picked up the new pain injections. If only I can get the courage to throw the needle into my leg. Although, we both have needle phobias, you are far worse." They both laugh.

The waitress returns with their food. After placing the plates piled high with salad in front of them, she asks if they need anything else. Mark gestures to his empty glass as Christina asks for two glasses. The waitress hurries away.

Christina looks at Mark intently and says, "I still can't believe Andrew would not just let you have your college fees. Now we are forced into mediation with Monika and we have to depose her first and of course pay more legal fees!"

"Get over it, Mom. If we can't change it, you need to stop worrying about it. It is what it is." Mark takes a mouthful of salad as Christina tells him, "I have no idea how you manage to stay so calm! Sergio is right. You are handling this better than most forty-year-olds would."

She is leaning on an elbow with a hand under her chin as she continues, "You turn eighteen soon and will become the official objector of this case. I will not be allowed to do it for you anymore. Remind me tomorrow that we need to do some prep, go over notes. We have to amend the objection to include the points on why we believe her will is forged, such as: the signature is not your dad's; the fact that he may also have been out of the country and could not have signed her will in Florida; as well as the obvious – Monika's *cut and paste* copied pages. You know, of course, that immediately after you become the objector they will depose you, probably even before we get to her deposition. They will try to find out just how much we know about her shenanigans. You'd better be prepared for all this."

Mark looks at his mother with concern. "Mom, you need to stop worrying. Believe me. I am ready for her and everything her cronies or attorneys are going to throw at me." Mark shifts in his seat. He stiffens his broad shoulders against the backrest just as the waitress returns with two large glasses of water. They thank her as she scurries off to the next table.

Mark’s mellow voice is interrupted briefly by the sound of distant fireworks seen through the window before he continues, “The legal system is really based on the almighty dollar. It doesn’t matter who is right or wrong, it’s based on how long you can drag out the case and pay the legal bills. We have really learned so much through all of this. When you die, your will doesn’t count for much since it can be disputed by anyone who thinks they have a claim. This has been a life lesson I will never forget. Really no-one would believe this unless you have experienced the system first-hand. You really need to safeguard your loved ones via life insurance and trust funds. Wills and Probate attorneys can’t touch those!”

Mark's grandmother (Yaya) and her new husband (Oupa) had nurtured the rose garden in front of their home on the conservation farm. Oupa was especially proud of the new red roses he had planted... until the herd of elephants decided they liked them too and trampled them on one of their walks. So, Oupa decided it was time to keep them away from the garden. The next time they came close he was going to use fireworks to

scare them off - Mark had strongly advised him against this. However, Oupa did not take advice well, especially from a 9 year old boy!

Oupa was going to prove his point and when alone at home one day while Yaya was at the restaurant, he let off the fireworks in the front garden, as the herd got close. Shortly afterwards, he was seen with Mark running from the back door of the house as the herd trampled the garden. The lead elephant bull threatened at least six runs at the house with his trunk held high and ears flapping furiously in response to this new loud noise. Luckily the house still stood, but the garden was not replanted. The lead elephant bull was often seen in the vicinity again. The locals believe that elephants never forget and especially not anyone who tried to harm their family herd. They would circle back to the house every now and again.

for the departed....

Chapter TEN

Christina is seated alone in a small North Palm Beach waiting area. Head down, she pages through a glossy magazine. Sunlight from the window behind her illuminates her highlighted hair and bounces off the room's sparse blue décor. Auto parts on the ledge behind her are indicators of an auto service center. Her cell phone rings and she has to uncross her legs to reach for it into her shorts pocket. Her mood is light.

She answers, "Hi, sweetie. Good, you got my message. Sergio called and said he had the date set for the mediation and Monika's deposition. No, I am still here. Well, I was on I-95 and the brake warning light kept coming on. Yes, good thing it did not happen on the Home Shopping trip. The light was still coming on this morning. I thought it was because of the heavy rains and the brakes were wet, but looks like it may be something else. So, I am having it checked out. Yep, I'm feeling much better today. Clear-headed, with no pain. How is school going? Oh, the service guy is here. I'll call you back."

The door to the room opens and a young man wearing dark blue overalls appears. His eyes are intense and his rugged face shows alarm. He seems a little shaken as he takes a few breaths before speaking. "Mrs. St. John, is there someone who wishes you harm?"

Christina is startled. She places the magazine on the table next to her and her cell phone back in her pocket. "Excuse me? Why?"

The mechanic still has one hand on the door handle. His feet are apart to steady the moment's impact when he tells her, "Well, we now know why your brake sensor warning light was permanently on. Someone cut three out of the four brake lines."

Christina's face says it all, her eyebrows rising, a visual aid for the disbelief in her voice. "You are not serious! You are? Well, they obviously did not know what they were doing - if they cut only three!" She is on her feet, her white blouse sticking to her chest, exposing a line of sweat. Her eyes glisten in the shock of the moment, quickly turning to anger.

The young man has not moved and still has his hand on the door handle. He opens his mouth to speak again. "Oh, they knew exactly what they were doing! I'd say this shows intent to kill and an attempt to make it look like an accident."

Christina is now closer to him. Her voice is low in anger. "If it is who I think it is, and it can only be, then they are pretty good at making something deliberate look like an accident."

He opens the door wide, gesturing with his free hand for Christina to join him outside. He continues. "They cut three lines instead of four. If you had applied your brakes at high speed, the force would have snapped the remaining line and you would either have gone into a spin or a roll over. Thank your guardian angels you got to us before anything happened. Come, let me show you. I have it up on the hydraulic lift. I've never come across anything like this - I've read about it, but never seen it."

Christina emerges into the harsh sunlight of the service yard and the young man finally lets go of the door handle, closing it behind her. She pulls down the sunglasses that were serving as a hair band and says to him, "I thank them every day. They were definitely watching out for us again. I had better call the police. Perhaps now someone will take our concerns with these crazy people seriously."

Walking toward the service lift, Christina dials 911 and asks for an officer to be sent to the service center's address after explaining her problem. She is told by dispatch that a patrolman is on his way.

She is now alongside the mechanic under her SUV. He points out the cut lines and she takes off her sunglasses, shaking her head in disbelief. "Wow! Never thought they would go this far. I suppose she figures she got away with the first incident, so why not make it a second or even a third! We are involved in a really bad lawsuit and we believe the new wife may very well have bumped off my son's father. Oh, my God! I'd better call my son. I hope his car is okay!"

She dials Mark's number and looks frustrated. He is not answering. She leaves a message after his voicemail prompts. "Mark, Mark. Do not get into your car. I hope I have caught you in time. I know you were leaving your last class when I had you on the phone. My brake lines were cut! The police are on the way. Please do not get into your car!" Just then a patrol car pulls into the service area and a uniformed, middle-aged man leaps out. Christina closes her flip cell phone and waves to show him their position. He walks toward them, his belted radio loudly active with a voice confirming his whereabouts.

The officer is sullen. His seriousness could be misjudged for disinterest. He introduces himself, shaking hands with both the mechanic and Christina. He moves directly under the car, looking up at the wheels. He shows no reaction other than a brief recognition in his eyes. He turns to the mechanic and they chat briefly, the mechanic verifying actual line cuts and the fact that three out of four brake lines are cut.

Christina has moved a safe distance away, allowing the patrolman to do his work. She is watching him expectantly as he approaches her. He is still a few steps away when she begins a nervous babble, "I am really worried about my son. He is the *real* target and would be the one they would want dead. We are going through a vicious litigation and we suspect the new wife could have killed his father and forged the will. In fact, we are confident she did, and that's why my car was sabotaged!"

The officer looks at her with an expressionless face and unclips his radio while asking her for Mark's whereabouts. He tells the dispatcher to get a patrol car to the suburban school and to check out the car of a student, Mark St. John. He clips the radio back onto his belt and turns his attention to her. "Okay, Mrs. St. John, let's draw up an official report. Then I'll head over to the school. We have two officers over there already"

He moves back to his patrol car and takes out a clipboard. He places it on his knee, sitting on the edge of the driver's seat, black boots on the service center's gravel driveway. He looks up at Christina, who is standing in front of him, arms folded. Her face is etched with controlled fear. He asks, "You say you think you know who could have done this. Has this person made a verbal threat on your life?"

Christina's reply shows her surprise. "I have no doubt the new wife in the will litigation is behind this. We have the Inspector General and even the FBI involved in Miami trying to prove the possible murder of my ex-husband. I will give you all their names and contact info. And there's the will, definitely forged…"

He interrupts her with some impatience. "Beyond the civil suit you are describing, has she threatened your life in a direct way?"

Christina looks shocked as she asks, "As in, 'I'm going to kill you'? You mean she actually has to verbally threaten me or you won't recognize this as attempted murder?"

The officer is taking notes and his reply is curt. "That's the law, ma'am."

She looks at him in disbelief. "You mean someone just cut my brake lines and if they didn't first threaten my life verbally, or tell me they were going to do this, it is not regarded as intent to kill?"

The officer shrugs his shoulders as he replies, "That's pretty much how it works!" Christina has grown impatient with the officer's comments and manner as she says, "I know the chief of police here and I will take the matter up with him. Obviously whoever did this knows the law too or they would not have managed to get away with this."

He looks startled at her outburst. "I'm going over to your son's school next. I have told the mechanic not to do any major repairs on your car until this is fully investigated."

Christina's cell phone rings and she reaches into her pocket. It is Mark saying, "Mom. The police are here and they think I may have a bomb in my car. They are checking it out and the school is going nuts! They really don't like the commotion. Yes, I got your message about the brake lines, but they are checking for everything."

Christina looks relieved. "I am so thankful they got to you in time. I have a patrolman with me. He is coming over and I will meet you there. Not sure if they will let me drive the car the way it is. I don't care about the school. They have a fit about anything that disturbs their pretentious façade! They should be worried about you. Life happens! And we cannot control the crazies in this world."

Mark replies, "I think the police are nearly done. Yes, they are walking toward me. I'll call you back."

She closes the flip phone but does not put it back into her pocket. In the interim the patrolman has roared off, wheels spinning. Christina looks after the disappearing car and walks toward the service area where her mechanic is showing the undercarriage to other mechanics.

The mechanics are all nodding and making comments. Christina looks at the young man, asking, "Can I drive it like this for now? Believe it or not, the officer does not want me to fix it yet!" The entire group looks on as he answers, "Sure thing, as long as you drive really slowly and go straight home on the side roads. Better still, I will drive behind you for safety sake."

Christina looks relieved and grateful. "Thank you very much. I was hoping to go pass my son's school first as well."

Just then the phone in her hand rings and she answers it quickly. It is Mark again. "Hey, Mom. Don't worry. Everything checked out - my car is fine. You don't need to come over. I'll meet you at home. Looks like she hates you more than me! " Both burst into relieved giggles, breaking the tension.

Christina replies, "That's odd. You are about to turn eighteen, and will be the official objector in the case. You would think she'd want both of us out of the way. I'm so glad you're safe. I'll see you at home, sweetie."

While she has been on the phone, the mechanics have lowered the SUV and are preparing to drive it into the driveway. She moves toward the car and thanks them all. She slides into the driver's seat with agility. The young mechanic motions to her to wait while he hops into his large white truck.

Christina is once again on her cell phone as she follows the truck into the afternoon traffic. The mechanic pulls his truck over as he waves for her to pass and go ahead. She passes him, waves a thank you and continues talking on her phone. “Hello, Lance. You are not going to believe this one - my brake lines were cut! Yep, she is really pissed off now and obviously wants us out of the way. I am on the way home and I’ve already filed a police report.”

Lance’s voice is filled with concern and disbelief. “Are you driving right now? I was on my way to the house anyway. I can pick you up.”

Her response is quick. “Oh, don’t worry. I have the mechanic following me. They said as long as I go slowly I will be okay.”

His voice is warm as he says, “I would really like to see you. I am sure you could do with a shoulder and a drink.” She laughs. “Yes, great idea, come over for a drink.” She closes her phone, cutting off his final words, “Love you, see you in …”

Christina’s smile begins to fade and her pallor returns. The tampering episode with her car’s brakes has left her shaken.

She keeps glancing into the rear-view mirror at the white truck following her. The drive is painstakingly slow before she finally turns into her gated community. She raises her arm out the window to wave her thanks to him. He waves back, makes a U-turn and leaves.

Driving through the community gates her smile returns as she notices Lance's car parked in front of her two-storey, peach-colored home. He sees her and grins. She pulls her car into the driveway and he opens her door. She steps out and Lance opens his arms to hug her, but he looks surprised. She has her arms crossed in front of her and gently pulls away saying, "It's been rough. Is Mark home yet?"

Lance looks hurt. "I don't think so. I tried the door and there was no answer. Hey, let me take a look under the car. I am finding all this hard to believe. Are you sure they didn't see a loose wire or something?" Her response is indignant as she says, "Take a look for yourself!"

Lance gets down on the driveway and slides under the car on his back. He stays there for a few minutes and as he slides back out Christina cannot hold back a smug grin in response to his amazed low whistle. He is wide-eyed and shocked. His only comment: “Hell! She really does want you dead.”

She replies, “Tell that to the police. The mere fact that neither Monika nor anyone in her group has threatened us verbally makes this a nonexistent attempt on our lives.”

Lance is sitting on his haunches next to the car. He looks up at her saying, “That’s absurd!”

Christina moves toward the front door and Lance stands to follow. He looks back at the car thoughtfully. “There’s no brake fluid on the driveway. It couldn’t have happened here.”

She looks at him with interest. “I didn’t think of that. It could have happened while I was shopping at the Palm Beach Gardens Mall yesterday. Funny, you know I always say you should follow your instincts. I had a strange feeling when I got back to the parking lot. There was a fair-haired, middle-aged guy walking hurriedly away from my car. He was glancing back at me nervously. I thought it might have been someone just looking into car windows to see what he could steal. I am beginning to realize I may have caught a glimpse of Monika’s new hit man, after he cut the brake lines.”

Lance asks, "Would you recognize him?" She is opening the front door as she says, "Maybe. But I really only saw him from the back. He had a medium-build, blond ponytail and probably middle aged."

Lance follows her into the dusk-lit house as he says, "Better remember those details and call the police with that information."

She pulls her mouth to the side sarcastically. "Yes, I am sure they're going to do something immediately on the strength of that description. I mean, he was not threatening me verbally, or anything as useful as that. I do need to call Mark's uncle about this and add this into his Inspector General report."

They walk into the kitchen and Lance reaches for the light switch as Christina opens the refrigerator door. She reaches for a bottle of wine and he opens a cupboard, taking out two glasses. They work together smoothly.

The front door bursts open and Mark's voice bellows through the foyer, "Hello, all! This time they have *got* to realize she is trying to kill everyone!" He strides into the kitchen, picks up his mother, swinging her around.

Christina laughs and says, "Put me down! Tell us what happened at school."

Mark has an excited look on his face as he launches into the story. "Oh! My God! It was a huge problem. Of course the students loved all the excitement. They think that because Dad was an African diplomat, that he probably has dangerous connections!"

Christina interjects, "Oh, great! Now we have to deal with that, too. Your father's bad choice in friends and new wife now causes a ripple effect in *THE* school of the area. For heaven's sake! I can only imagine what the celebrity families will think! And let's not forget all the attorney parents as well."

Mark laughs. "Don't worry, Mom. All their kids are just like me. We have a good understanding of our parents and our lives. I know the principal was not happy the police were there. He is obviously more worried about what the other parents may think, especially the big donor ones." Christina laughs.

Lance has poured the glasses of wine and hands an additional one to Mark with a wink, saying, "I am sure no one will mind. Here, you may need this."

Mark smiles as he takes the glass and gulps down a few sips. Christina picks up the phone on the counter saying, “I should call Uncle Andrew now and let him know about the newest developments.”

Both men pull up bar stools at the kitchen counter. They start chatting excitedly about the day’s events while listening to Christina’s telephone comments, reacting to them occasionally with a nod and knowing wink at each other. “Yes, Andrew, that is exactly what they said. They can’t investigate the Miami crowd about my sabotaged brakes unless we have had a direct, life-threatening declaration. Yes, I know that’s ridiculous. Yes, I was hoping you would. If you add this into the Inspector General’s new report perhaps that will force someone to do something. I know - in the meantime we wait for her to try again! We’ll have absolutely no protection. Of course it’s bizarre!”

Christina looks over at Mark as she takes in a deep breath through clenched teeth. She then changes the direction of the telephone conversation, “So, the latest step here in the legal case is that we did hear from our attorney and the mediation date, as well as her deposition date, is set. I am going to contact that friend of ours, the one whose husband is the chief of police in this area. Anyway, it is clear that Monika does not want to be deposed or go to trial. Just wants us to go away - literally!"

Mark whispers to his mom, "Ask him what the Inspector General has said so far."

"Andrew, Mark wants to know what the Inspector General has said - if anything." She looks at Mark as she repeats Andrew's reply, "Oh - they will look into it." Mark rolls his eyes in response. Christina ends her call, saying she will call back the next day.

She has no sooner replaced the receiver than it rings again and the voice on the other end says, "Mrs. St. John?"

Christina replies with, "That would be me."

The voice on the phone line continues, "This is Janet Wiseman, the Jermaine School's secretary. Mr. Phillips, our principal would like to speak with you." Christina repeats the sentence for Mark's benefit and her voice is tinged with disdain. "Oh, Mr. Phillips, the school principal, wants to speak to me!"

The voice replies with a cold, "Yes."

Christina hits the speakerphone button with a fingernail and moves from her spot at the granite kitchen countertop to the bar stool next to Mark. She stares straight ahead with icy coldness in her eyes and says: “Okay, I will speak with him!”

A cold, Southern-accented male voice is heard on the phone speaker. “Mrs. St. John, I do need to speak to you about the current situation with Mark. We were displeased with the commotion today and of course not happy with Mark’s grades over the last few months. We may have no alternative but to ask him to leave the school and finish his last few months of high school elsewhere.”

Christina looks down at the countertop, avoiding Mark’s questioning look as she replies in a tougher, even-toned voice. It is obvious she is preparing to vent the day’s frustrations on this caller, as she launches into an unstoppable ramble.

“Mr. Phillips, how are you? I think this was something you regrettably forgot to open our conversation with. Anyway, let me make myself perfectly clear. I am extremely offended that you would be more worried about a commotion than you are about the life of one of your students. Even more disconcerting is the fact that you are considering letting him go shortly before the final exams of his senior year - the most important exams of his school life. We, like other families, have paid your exorbitant private school fees over the past few years, but I think what upsets me most is your unbelievable cold-heartedness. As you know, Mark's father died a few months ago and he has been launched into a lawsuit that most 40 year olds would not know how to deal with. Of course his grades have dropped! He is still grieving for his father. But you know what, I will make sure to help him get some extra tutoring to get his grades back up I am quite sure he will make your school proud and will be accepted into a good college. If you try to force him to leave I will be sure to have this matter in a lawyer's hands before the end of the week and of course in every local newspaper I can find. So, now, Mr. Phillips, if you need anything else, tell me right now!"

Mark and Lance are both listening intently. They are staring at Christina's face with a mix of pride and fright. The male voice on the phone is silent but his annoyed breathing is heard clearly. His voice is far less aggressive and even sheepish, as he answers, "No Oh, that is fine. Thank you, Mrs. St. John.

Well, as long as Mark's grades are back up to par quickly that will be fine. Goodbye, Mrs. St. John. Have a nice evening."

She replies curtly. "No! I wish to thank *you* Mr. Phillips. Goodbye." Christina replaces the phone, hitting the speaker button a little too harshly. Her face looks drained by this last blow. She looks beaten in spirit as she speaks to the two men staring at her. "Okay, that's it. Sorry guys, I feel one of those headaches starting, I need to go and rest. A dark room and heating blanket on the neck will be the only way."

Christina turns sharply on her heel and walks toward the stairs as Lance calls out after her, "Is there anything I can get for you? I can go to the store." She looks at him over her shoulder. "Sorry, Lance, I really need to chill out. I probably just need to be alone and in a cool, dark room. It is all too much to deal with. I'll call you tomorrow."

Lance tries to mask his disappointment. "Sure. I'll finish my drink and maybe make Mark dinner?"

Mark looks at him and just like his mother says, "Sorry, Lance, I am beat also. I am really not hungry at all. Thanks for the offer."

Lance looks uncomfortable. He pours out the balance of his drink into the kitchen sink, places it on the counter and says, Well, I'd better get going. If you need anything, let me know."

Christina looks at him, touched by the awkwardness of the moment. She decides to follow him out onto the patio where she gives him a peck on the cheek. Lance looks a little more reassured. "I suppose you have had it from all sides today. Have a good rest Christina. I will check in with you in the morning. Bye for now. Stay safe."

Mark looks at his mother as she walks back into the house and toward the stairs. "Can I get you some ice, Mom?" She looks at him with gratitude. "Yes, thanks, sweetie. That always helps. What are you going to do tonight?" She continues up the stairs as Mark replies.

"Nothing more than watch some TV and sleep. Don't worry, Mom. I will get my grades back up. Everything will look better in the morning. What are you going to do about Lance? Poor guy. He must be feeling in the way, with all this going on."

Christina looks over the banister at him with a warm smile, "I know, my boy, I know. Lance is a good guy, but we are on a roller-coaster ride and there's no way he will be able to help. He may get caught up in a dangerous situation. I am going to have to call him tomorrow and break things off."

Mark replies, "Yes, you never know. Wrong place, wrong time and something could happen. You don't look too good, Mom. Are you really okay? I am putting some ice in a bag for you and I'll bring it up. Did you check the phone messages?"

She turns and slowly climbs the stairs, as she replies, "No Could you check them?"

Mark presses the speakerphone button and begins to listen to the messages. He loudly empties some ice from the fridge into a plastic bag, and stops dead as he hears Sergio's voice echo through the kitchen. "Well, here we go. Mrs. Monika Fischer Levine St. John would like to depose you, Mark… and your father's files have miraculously and suddenly appeared, according to her attorney!"

Mark grins and moves quickly upstairs, ice bag in hand. "Hey, Mom, you are not going to believe this! Well, actually, you probably will."

Mark's caring nanny, Ester, is brushing his hair neatly into a side path. The 5 year old is in his well-pressed school uniform. They are both standing in front of the coal fire heater which is encased in a wooden carved fireplace. It is a large room built of red brick with steel pressed ceilings.

Christina walks in asking if they are warm enough and if Mark is ready for school. She comments on it being a chilly Johannesburg winter morning just as a dog is heard barking furiously in the back garden. All three run towards the barking, down the passage and through the kitchen. They peer through the window. Their black Labrador is in a face-off with a green snake that is ready to strike. Ester's husband, Robert, is yelling from a distance at the dog with the garden spade in hand. It is clear he is trying to get the dog to back off from an inevitable fight that no-one can win.

Ester's actions are swift. She grabs for the kitchen broom, charges outside directly for the snake. She then proceeds to beat the snake with the broom handle until motionless. Robert backs her up with the spade and cuts off its head.

Christina and Mark watch in disbelief at the bravery and quick actions of their loyal nanny and her husband, who is also their landscaper.

Ester holds up the writhing body of the green snake with pride. Robert says is it most definitely a Green Mamba, one of the most poisonous snakes in Africa.

angry warriors…

Chapter ELEVEN

In the prestigious attorney's boardroom, the occupants are dwarfed by the oversized dark mahogany table flanked by high-backed black leather chairs. A row of etched crystal glasses and a decanter are displayed on the matching mahogany side credenza.

Monika and her attorney, Kurt, are seated opposite Mark and Christina with their attorney, Sergio. The latter is adjusting his overweight midriff into his trouser belt as inconspicuously as possible. Kurt greets them in an eloquent tone, hinting at his experience in trial law. His expensively- tailored, dark gray suit accentuates his red hair; his exposed crisp white monogrammed sleeve cuffs frame his tanned wrists.

Sergio looks at the papers in front of him, nervously fingering the edges. He occasionally glances up at Mark and Christina, then across at Monika with a knowing look over his rimless spectacles. His bald head reflects the glare of the overhead office spotlights. There is a slight, sarcastic smile at the corners of his mouth. The reason for his amusement seems to be Monika's ensemble for the day. She is dressed in a classic gray double-breasted suit. Her hair is coiled neatly in an up-do and her ears are decorated with modest white single-pearl earrings. She appears to be very satisfied with her new look.

Christina has noticed Sergio's bemused reaction to Monika's new look. They are both trying to suppress laughter. Giggling, Christina excuses herself from the gathering with her hand over her mouth as she stands, revealing a Ralph Lauren crisp black linen skirt suit and white blouse. She has her usual up -do and pearl earrings. After a few minutes she reappears in the doorway, more composed.

Mark is casually dressed in his tennis clothes. His fidgeting takes the form of swiveling in the leather armchair. In between statements Kurt glares at Mark's side-to-side motion with annoyance, saying with sarcasm, "Well, finally, we reached an agreed date for your deposition, Mr. St. John."

Sergio replies for Mark. "Kurt, give it a break. He has school. Saturday is the only day suitable. The school is having a real problem with this case and the absences it has caused. You know the judge will have issue with that. He has even managed to be here after a school tennis match today."

Kurt looks unimpressed as he continues, "Okay, then let's carry on. You've given me all the basics - address, Social Security and so on, but let's cut to the chase. You have filed a very serious objection against my client, Mrs. Fischer Levine St. John, in regard to the will she has produced. What do you base this on? If anything at all?"

Mark stops his fidgeting and looks directly at Kurt, happy at last to have his time to speak. "My father would never have put together a will like that. It's unprofessional. Let me give it to you as bullet points: Number one: My father was an astute and meticulous businessman and would never have signed such an amateurish document. It appears to be a paste-up! Number two: He was left-handed and wrote with a sharply cocked wrist that did not allow him to make some letters rounded. As a result, he had a very distinctive signature. This is definitely not his signature. Number three: This goes to content. He would never have cut his mother or me out of his will. At the time this will was dated, he was still supporting his mother, my grandmother, in a Canadian nursing home. I was a young, dependent child and he was also supporting me through child support. My father would never have abandoned either of us. Number four: He would never have made a mere business acquaintance, Alain du Pont, the original personal representative of his entire estate. Number five: There are conflicting stories as to how and where your client's will was executed. Number six: There is confusion as to where it was found. And last but not least, number seven: My father may very well have been out of the country when this will was dated and signed. He could not have been in two places at the same time."

Christina barely manages to suppress a gasp of proud elation; their hard work has paid off. Mark has presented a calm, organized, persuasive argument.

Kurt's hand reaches for his tie and seems to be loosening the knot as he focuses on Mark's last statement, which has obviously piqued his interest. "I am well aware of that truism, young man. No one can be in two places at once! But what proof do you have that your father was out of the country? This all seems very far-fetched!"

Mark responds to him with a slight smile and says, "Am I not going to be questioned about the first six points I gave you?"

Kurt looks annoyed. "I am asking the questions here. I will repeat myself. What proof do you have that he was not in the country?"

Mark grins confidently. He places his forearms on the table with his right fist under his chin before answering, "Well, from the Modification of Child Support agreement signed by my mother and father. There is a fax imprint at the top with a phone number. This was on the same date that his new wife, Monika Fischer Levine St. John, claims he was in Florida signing her alleged will. This was the fax number of a Pennsylvania hotel where he was attending a business seminar. From there he went on to Canada to celebrate my cousin's twenty-first birthday. We are waiting for the hotel records to verify exact dates."

Monika looks startled and Kurt looks across at her with reassurance before he continues. "So, where is this agreement? You sound unsure. Clarify! Also, please stop using all my client's prior married and maiden last names."

Sergio looks up from his papers. It is clear he has been paying close attention. "Objection! Asked and answered! You know Mark has already answered that question. You are already in possession of the modification agreement. This was part of the discovery I sent to you. There is nothing to clarify. Also, *you* are the one who began this meeting mentioning all your client's last names."

Kurt and Monika shuffle their documents nervously around on the table and find the agreement in question, and they both peer closely at the fax imprint at the top. Kurt looks at Mark saying, "You are referring to this...?"

Mark drops his fist from under his chin and leans back comfortably in the chair. He answers confidently and calmly. "Yes, and we are waiting for the hotel records to arrive. We know from my Uncle Andrew that my dad was in Toronto on the 24th or 25th. His journey ended in Ottawa by the 28th in time for his niece's 21st birthday. Numerous witnesses can put him there. As I said, he could not be in two places at the same time. There is no way he could have been in Florida signing Monika's will."

Kurt replies with an aggressive question. "Are you then accusing the signatory witnesses on my client's will of lying?"

Mark remains un-rattled by the attack. "I am undecided what to accuse them of at this stage, Mr. Dubb. Only after we have done our full discovery will we know what they did or did not do."

Sergio's head is cocked to the side and he answers quickly. "Give it a break, Kurt, you know full well we are still in our discovery stage and if you would not keep objecting via your numerous court petitions against everything we try to discover, maybe we would be further along by now. We'll depose the signing witnesses on that will and believe me, we will find them! Unlike Richard's so-called missing files which have suddenly been found. I believe *your* office handed them over to the curators? "

Kurt looks down at his notes as he tries to recover his composure. "The files were dropped off at our offices, and we have no way of knowing who dropped them. Richard's office cabinets had been forced open by persons unknown before those files disappeared. Anyway, who is deposing whom here?"

Mark, Christina and Sergio look at him with the same contemptuous look of disbelief. No one bothers to reply.

Kurt changes the conversation by reclaiming his attack role. “And I fully intend deposing your document examiner.”

Sergio replies, “Better yet, I'll tell you what. This is the second examiner. We are so confident of our results on forgery that I will invite you to be present during his examination at my offices. How is that?”

Kurt answers quickly, “Yes, I will definitely be there for this examination. Where is the report from the first one?”

Sergio looks at him calmly. “There was no report, just an initial examination, but we felt because of the questions raised on your client’s will, it warranted a second examination from an FBI-based forgery examiner.”

Kurt shrugs and turns his attention back to Mark, then in an increasingly abrasive tone says, “Then of course we have this absurd and irresponsible accusation you have been throwing around in public that you *think* your stepmother may have had something to do with your father’s death. I mean, really, Mr. St. John! Do you understand the legal definitions of slander and defamation? You are accusing my client of an unfounded criminal offense."

Mark twists his frame in his chair to look directly at Monika for the first time. Monika avoids Mark's stare and looks down at the table top waiting for his reply.

Mark does not take his eyes off her as he answers in a steely tone. "Yes, I do think that my father's wife, Mrs. Monika Levine Fischer St. John, not only had something to do with my father's death, but orchestrated it. In fact, I have no doubt my father was murdered." Mark has not shown any intimidation, but seems to have welcomed the chance to voice his belief. His delivery is so convincing that even Kurt looks shocked. The latter's demeanor has turned from controlled cynicism to concerned doubt.

Kurt regains his composure and asks quickly, "Why do you keep calling your stepmother by all those names? Do you realize that making defamatory, injurious statements is slander? There is absolutely no proof of this, with absolutely no criminal investigation in process. On what do you base this far-fetched accusation, young man?"

Mark replies without hesitation still looking directly at Monika who is visibly shaken. She is still looking down at the table. "First, she is not and has never been my stepmother. She was my father's wife. Second, I am using all the names she is using within all her own legal documentation supplied to us. Some are her maiden names and prior married names. I have added my father's name to the end of the list. It appears that she is the one not sure of which name to use now. Interestingly, she does not seem to want to carry my father's name. Last, we have ample proof: money as a motive; a forged will; and conflicting accident witness reports."

Monika, startled, looks up at Mark with a sinister glare. Sergio interjects quickly, "Kurt, today's deposition is supposed to be about the probate. If you want to deal with other allegations we will have to move forward with filing a criminal case. I am sure your client is not ready for that right now. Please redirect your questioning."

Kurt takes a quick look at Monika whose facial muscles are pulled taught in defiance. He tries once again to reassure her with his eyes as he says in his caustic voice, "Okay, then, let's give it a break. My client's deposition date is set for next week. We thought we would make it easier on everyone by allowing the estate curators to depose her first, then you can do round two. We will see you all again then. Sergio, you will let me know when you intend to examine the will, so I can be there.... and of course when you will be considering our settlement offers?"

Sergio says agreeably, "Sure." It is obvious that he is satisfied with the meeting. They all stand. Mark and Christina leave the room first, thanking Kurt politely for his time but ignoring Monika completely. Sergio shakes both Kurt's and Monika's hand before he leaves.

Sergio walks quickly to catch up to Christina and Mark who are holding the elevator door for him. He readjusts his belt again, bounces in and looks up at Mark towering above him. "Well done, young man. You did extremely well. Only told them what they asked and the minimal amount they needed to know. He was the one stupid enough not to ask more questions related to the wills. He made the mistake of bringing up the subject of Richard's death, not you. It's interesting that Kurt avoided all your responses other than your father's trip. It looks like he is beginning to worry that Monika has not been entirely truthful. Did you see her face as the subject of murder came up? It's also really interesting that he mentioned the settlement offers again immediately after that."

Mark is smiling with relief and confidence as he says, "You didn't expect her to be truthful with her attorney or anyone else for that matter, did you, Sergio?"

Sergio laughs as he responds, "Yeah, I suppose that would be expecting too much. I can't wait to get our hands on your father's files. I am sure we may very well find proof of money elsewhere in the world, and of course the credit card receipts that will show he was out of the country when Monika claims he was here signing her will."

As they step out of the elevator and walk through the executive office lobby, Mark asks, "Do we know how long the estate curators may keep Dad's files? Or, should I say, what's left of them, now that she has had several months to go through them. She would have already found documentation of any money or assets elsewhere in the world. I would assume she would have taken it all by now. Why else would she have pretended not to have them - before suddenly giving them over to the attorneys?"

Sergio looks at him. "That may be a question for your uncle. The estate attorneys may keep them for as long as they can. That allows them to charge more."

Christina looks at her watch as they stand on the sidewalk before she says, "Sergio, it is lunchtime. We can buy you a quick bite before we head back. We need to go through a few things and can't keep coming down every few days. It's not only bad for Mark's school grades, but my business is suffering."

Sergio answers. "Of course, there is a nice little Cuban restaurant on the corner. Still can't believe what you told me the other day - that Monika and I share the same birthday!" Christina raises an eyebrow, showing concern with his last remark.

The three head down the street and Mark directs a comment at Sergio, "She learns fast. Did you see what she was wearing today? She is trying hard to look more professional and is even dressing just like my mother. You know, many of my father's friends even used to say she looks just like a mini-me of my mother."

Christina looks horrified. "Oh, God, no, you have got to stop saying that. But, it is certainly interesting how she has changed her style for this case."

Sergio is smiling and holding the restaurant door open for Christina as he looks toward the street and says, "Hey, take a look at that Porsche. Mine will be yellow. As for Mrs. Monika Fischer Levine St. John's new look. I'm sure her attorney had something to do with that. He wants the judge to have a better impression of her. She was not doing very well with that before."

As they enter the restaurant, they all laugh at Sergio's mention of all Monika's names again. Mark looks around for a table as an elderly woman comes hurrying up. Sergio speaks to her in Spanish and she happily ushers them to a wooden table covered with plastic.

Mark takes a deep breath. "It smells really good in here." Sergio's reply takes full credit for the choice of restaurant. "Wait till you taste the food. Let me suggest the chicken, beans and fried plantains."

Mark responds with, "Sounds good to me, I am famished and love plantains." They take their seats and Sergio pulls out his notepad from a leather folio. He is first to speak. “Let's see where we are now. We have had three settlement offers from them, the last one in the mediation, which we have ignored. But let us reiterate. Monika wants to walk away from her sole claim to the estate; she will share control with you based on a payoff. It is clear they do not want to go to trial. We finally got a copy of Richard’s earlier will and Monika’s pre-nup from the attorney Richard used in preparing both before he died. They filed objection after objection to try to stop that one. You have to wonder why. Anyway, the will does appear to be an original and the one that Richard legitimately left behind with his family attorney. Our problem of course is that the one she has submitted, the forged one, has the later date. The law allows only the latest dated will to stand.”

Sergio notices the look of disappointment on Mark’s face. He shifts in his seat and directs the rest of his statement to Mark. “Mark, it is important to know that you have been right. Your father did not cut you or his mother out and even included your illegitimate sister. However, he did cut Monika out completely, which must have pissed her off enough to agree to the forgery. It does look like they had a copy of the real will when your father died; they used the copy as a working model and changed it around to make their own. We could see the evidence of 'cut and paste.' It also seems to be the same content as the second will sent to Andrew from someone saying he was Richard's friend. Whoever sent that knew that a forgery had been placed into probate by Monika and was trying to expose it."

Seeing some relief in Mark's face, Sergio continues confidently. "Remember, the pre-nup confirms she was only supposed to receive a car, a few thousand dollars and the life insurance policy - which we know she wasted no time in cashing out. Obviously, this wasn't enough for her. I know much of this seems to be leaning our way. However, I have got to tell you that you do need to consider settling …"

Both Christina and Mark interrupt him with the same angry retort. "Absolutely not!"

Mark crosses his arms and scowls at Sergio. Christina has stiffened and her eyes flash angrily. "I refuse to believe that we have come this far and have got this much evidence and have to settle."

Mark adds, “Are you saying I have to settle with the woman who I know had something to do with my father’s death? Who also made my life a living hell as long as they were married?!? My mother has practically lost her house and her business in order to keep paying you. They are intentionally dragging us to this crap in Miami, only to wear us down financially. ”

Sergio seems unfazed by their reaction. He leans back confidently in his chair. “Let’s be practical. You need to consider settling. Not only are you starting to find it difficult to pay me but the estate is being raped by the curator's attorneys, and I include your Uncle Andrew in that. Doesn’t he keep getting his curator fees paid each month? They keep saying they have a long way to go with the documents and files before they can file the closing tax forms. There will be nothing left for anyone, not even for my own fees as well as outstanding percentage of the estate, or funds for Mark’s schooling, or to settle your own debts, my dear Christina.”

Christina frowns scornfully at him. She is obviously annoyed with his sarcasm and attempts to placate her. Mark is sitting next to Sergio, who cannot see him motioning to Christina with his eyes – in an attempt to calm her reaction. She looks at Mark and realizes she must not overreact. Instead, her reply is stoic and controlled. "I can't blame Andrew St. John. He's just not savvy enough. He is still thinking like a Canadian and believes the entire legal system is still a controlled profession, not realizing that parts of it have become a gluttonous business. Especially the wills and probate areas."

Sergio retorts with a sneer, "Oh, I beg to differ. It is still a profession, albeit one that has to be run as a business."

Christina answers in her most composed voice. "It is still a business and one of the major businesses in Florida, unlike other States within the US where attorneys are still professionals. Also, attorneys' billing practices in many other countries are controlled and they can even get taken to court if they overcharge - their bills get vetted by a judge. In Florida, attorneys are the law. You even have to have the actual attorney agree to the dispute against him by a client, before you can file a complaint with the Bar Association! Remember, we have lived in and visited many other countries and know the difference."

The waitress is back with their food. She is balancing three plates along her forearm and utensils in the other hand. It is a welcome break in the rising tension at the table. The plates of food are placed in front of them. They pick up their utensils simultaneously. Mark is first to begin to eat.

Sergio holds his knife and fork base-down on the table in an almost threatening manner. He looks at Christina over his spectacles, saying: “Christina, this is the greatest legal system in the world and the greatest country to be an attorney in.”

Christina is about to take a mouthful of food but before she does, she replies, “So I am continuously told, especially by attorneys. In fact, if you don’t have an attorney in the family with at least that sense of loyalty, you don’t stand a chance as a normal citizen. For heaven’s sake, Sergio, the highest level of our government is almost all made up of attorneys. Every second President is an attorney. This is no longer a democracy. What happened to the idea of a government made up of different people and different professions? They just keep passing laws to ensure the legal system remains a business and this basically ruins the average citizen’s life.”

Mark looks at his mother. He is chewing a mouthful of food and shakes his head again at her. She nods as discreetly as possible and there is an awkward silence for a few minutes. Mark reaches into his shirt pocket changing the subject as he says, “Sergio, I brought this to show you.”

Sergio is looking agitated as he glances at the clip of a newspaper advertisement Mark is unfolding on the table. Mark points to a few lines, saying, “There is little doubt Monika is getting desperate. Look at this ad. She is trying to sell Richard’s farm. As you can see it is listed for $ 1.4 million. I know the paperwork on the farm is complicated, but it should still stay in the estate. That's probably why my father formed that second-mortgage dummy corporation on the farm, to keep it away from Monika. No doubt, just in case they got divorced.”

Sergio looks refocused. His demeanor is more at ease as he comments, “That is tricky, but she would have to pay that large second mortgage if we did not allow her to have it in a settlement. I’ll hang onto this and chat with the estate attorneys. I am sure they would want it to stay in the estate too. This all hinges on that document examiner and the forgery evidence.

Then of course they will hire one who will say the will is not a forgery. Our expert is not an independent, and works with the FBI, so he is far more credible and would never accept payment to lie." Mark nods and asks the waitress for a glass of water. Sergio seizes the opportunity and says, "Talking about payment, I need another payment on my bill from you. I just can't keep carrying this case financially. I hope you understand."

Christina pushes her plate away and Mark does the same simultaneously. Their food remains unfinished. She crosses her arms saying," You are not serious. You have taken everything I have and you were just bragging about buying a yellow Porsche! Your first question when we first hired you was how much we could give you as a retainer. In fact, it was based on how much money we had available and you wanted it all, not some clearly defined amount appropriate for a case like this. You took all, and I mean all, of Mark's minimal life insurance policy his father had allocated in our divorce agreement. Then you started taking everything I have. I can't pay you. I am about to lose my house not because of Monika, but because of you!"

Sergio leans back in his chair and crosses his arms. "I am not carrying this case!"

Christina is furious. "What exactly have you done besides answer a few letters make a few phone calls and show up at the occasional hearing? We are doing all the work for the discovery, which you say you are too busy to do. We are hiring the PI, whom we found, something you say you cannot do. All you are doing is making calls and making sure there *are* more and more hearings! It is absurd that attorneys are allowed complete billing freedom, charging more than $400 to $1000 per hour plus expenses. Added to this will be a percentage of the estate settlement for you! The legal and financial system is going to cripple the country one day. It is insane!"

Sergio's face is hardening and his brown eyes turn black as he says, "I work hard for you and have not billed you for half of it." Mark is quiet, looking at both of them fearfully. This has been a long time coming and he is allowing both sides to vent.

Christina's voice rises as she replies, "You have double-billed us on numerous occasions. Then you purposely don't take our calls, making sure we have got to call back. Each call gets billed for, even if we speak to your receptionist. God help us if we question the bill! You charge us for asking about that too! It is unethical and it has got to stop! Why aren't we going to trial? Why are you dragging this out?"

It is clear Mark knows his mother well and recognizes that her new tone may lead to a louder escalation. He decides to jump in. "Mom. Hold on, Sergio. What exactly is the hold-up? What problems prevent us from going to trial? It seems we have more than enough to take this to trial. All we are waiting for is the document examiner's final report and the proof that Dad was out of the country when he was supposed to be signing her forged will. We should be able to go to trial in the next couple of months."

Christina stands as she takes $50 in cash out of her purse, throws it on the table and then hangs her handbag over her shoulder, saying with an icy voice tinged with contempt, "Our problem with this is obvious. Our attorney is trying to get whatever he can as this all ends and has become extremely busy with other cases. I have drained everything I have to pay the legal bills to get us to this point. This is a rotten system! You can murder your spouse, forge a will, throw it into the system, and if we do not have enough money to prove our side over a period of drawn-out litigation, then the guilty party wins? Just look at the OJ case. He got away with murder because the system stinks! He had the money to pay for two or three of the best attorneys and they manipulated the jury pool and turned it into a racial issue. The dollar *is* the deciding factor between winners and losers."

Sergio looks up at her as he pushes his chair back. He folds his arms defensively across his puffed-up chest and says flatly, "The system works. If we move to go to trial now, we may be given a date a year from now, and that gives the estate attorneys, as well as your Uncle Andrew, all the time in the world. I know you trust him, but he has done little to help you. Has he given you a dime or tried to arrange for the estate to give Mark his college fees? No! He has done absolutely nothing. All he does is direct you to do the research, find out things about the witnesses or the forgery or whatever, and he does nothing. He is the one who keeps taking money out of the estate in his curator's fees as long as he can keep things going."

Mark intervenes quickly. He clearly is expecting an explosive confrontation between his mother and their attorney. Their voices are rising and people at other tables are turning around to locate the source of the commotion.

At this stage the ensuing argument is volatile but still controlled as Mark says, “Okay, let's get back to what we can and cannot do. You said Monika's attorney is sending another settlement offer. I can’t believe I have to settle with the woman who murdered my father because of legal fees - yours as well as those of the estate attorneys. But I know this has destroyed my mother’s life and now threatens my future. But okay, let's take a look at her offer. It may be the only way for all of us to get on with our lives, get rid of the estate attorneys and pay you. Better the devil you know, I suppose. Oh! By the way, we made contact with Doreen, Dad’s secretary in the Toronto office. She said she picked him up at the Toronto airport when he went to my cousin’s 21st birthday. This trip followed onto his Pennsylvania visit. She slept with him the same night at a hotel and is willing to testify that his flight came in from Pennsylvania. Obviously, they were having an affair.”

Sergio looks surprised as the three rise to leave the restaurant. As they emerge into the afternoon sunlight he says, "Now we're talking. Why didn't you mention this before? Can you get the affidavit? This could turn things around completely with this case. We will then have conclusive proof of not only the documents, but a witness to the fact he was not in Miami signing their will, but in Toronto!"

Mark shakes Sergio's hand. Christina has begun to walk away but stops and looks back at them, saying, "Affair? Affairs, plural! Monika's ego would never allow her to think Richard would cheat on her. He thought he'd found the perfect wife - a stupid, self-absorbed one who couldn't see beyond the end of her nose. Only thing he missed seeing was that she did not love him, only his money. To answer your question: Yes, Doreen has agreed to give us an affidavit. She wants to do the right thing and is a good person. I never blamed her or any of the others. He was always the seducer. He just could not control himself. I believe it is now considered sexual addiction. We wanted something in writing from Doreen before we told anyone – even you."

Christina turns sharply away and puts on her sunglasses to hide her angry tears. She does not look back again as Sergio waves a goodbye to them both. Mark follows his mother silently to the parking garage.

They reach the car and Christina turns to him saying, "We had better call Andrew and figure out what he has in the files from your father's office and when we can actually get them. And by the way, the legal system does stink!"

He laughs at her. "I know, Mom. I know and you are not going to change it. It has already changed our lives - and us!"

Mark takes the keys out of his mother's hands and gets into the driver's seat. She hops into the passenger side, opening her flip phone as she closes the door. She leaves a voicemail for Andrew as Mark asks, "Not there? Make sure to tell him we must speak to him tonight." Christina follows suit. Mark peers through the windscreen at the sky as they enter the street. He continues. "A storm is brewing. We always seem to drive through storms to, or from Miami."

"Yes, that's got to mean something...." Just then her cell phone rings. She flips it open, putting it to her ear without looking at the caller ID. “Hi Andrew! Yes, Mark did extremely well. Her attorney was even stupid enough to go into the murder side of things and Mark said outright that he felt she had something to do with Richard’s death. Yes, I know. I am proud of him, too. He handled it well. Sorry, this line is bad. I didn’t hear that. We are driving through a bad storm. Oh. Yes, Sergio told us you finally have Richards's files. How intact are they?”

She looks across at Mark as she repeats the last sentence. “I am not surprised there are some empty files and that key files are missing. Are the credit card receipts there? Well, that’s not a surprise. Most of those around the time they dated the will would disappear. But what about any travel receipts? Good, some of them may help. Yes, we knew she tried to get her hands on the money in Zurich before the estate attorneys did. Oh, that was stupid of her to leave some notes on the calls she made to the bank. Stupid and funny. Yes, we knew he had some eighty registered companies, but you know, of course, there were only two of those that could be described as active. He used to register names he liked just to hold on to them, but never actually ran any active business under them. He’d drop the names when he decided he didn't want to use them. Sorry, I missed that. Please repeat that."

Christina's eyes are large as she looks across at Mark who glances back, taking his eyes off the road for a few seconds. "The estate attorneys are going to investigate each one, even though they are inactive? And you agreed to that? Well, I am sorry, Andrew. You are not right, they are not right. There is absolutely nothing there if they are registered as inactive with the state. You can't believe that! Of course they are going to say that. They have to. They are trying to prolong the estate so they can take it all! Have your attorneys given you any indication of how long it will take to go through the files? What? Absolutely no idea? I would like to get my hands on them as soon as possible. I can barely hear you, Andrew. Sorry, it's the storm. What was that? Yes, we did bring up the fact that we knew she'd had the files for the past six or seven months and was lying about someone else taking them."

Christina finishes the call with a deep sigh that is barely audible above the torrential rain. She looks at Mark. "This is a bad storm. Don't you want to pull over? I can't see a thing through the windscreen."

Mark looks at her and his answer seems to carry a great deal of meaning as he says, "We'll be fine. We have been through worse before. Did Lance call today?"

She looks at him and sighs again. "No. I had to make the call that I have been putting off. I made it last night. He needs to get on with his life now and so do we. This saga has made us grow apart. He just can't connect to any of this."

Mark looks at her and comments, "How did he take it?"

Christina looks over at him. She notices his sad eyes focused through the windshield and says, "He knew it was coming. He said he would still be there if we needed him. I think that was very sweet of him."

As they pass under a bridge overhang that punctuates the storm's noise with a brief interruption, Mark sums up their day. "Well, we are still in the game. She really thought that with the extra pressure and hiring the best attorneys from a large firm, then trying to kill you by cutting your brake lines…we would be scared off. She didn't realize just how formidable we could be.

It is a funny thing though. I don't seem to hate her or feel sorry for her at all. It's kind of weird, but I feel absolutely nothing for her, good or bad."

"Yes, that is ironic. I feel the same way. Absolutely no feelings for her one-way or the other. It's almost as though she does not exist and we are only fighting the system. I don't really even feel her presence in the room. It is almost as though she is not there or she is just an empty shell. Probably better this way. She really is not worth any feelings or any of our energy."

Christina drops her head back onto the headrest, saying, "I am so proud of you. You handled things very well today. Thanks for being the adult."

Mark smiles and says jokingly, "One of us needs to be! You know Dad used to say that the only sure thing in life is that you die."

Christina smiles as she closes her eyes. "It's a good thing you had the chance to speak to him a few days before he went to Key Largo. You said he didn't really want to go to Key Largo - he'd hoped to go to the farm in Ocala?"

"Yes. He said it was Monika's idea to go to Key Largo. One of his friends said they had been fighting badly and she suggested the weekend reconciliation in the Keys."

Christina rolls her head on the headrest to look at him and says, "I am going to close my eyes for a few minutes. I am really tired. Are you okay to drive?"

Mark looks across at her with a smile. "You mean without your watching me? I'm fine. You'd better rest, Mom."

Mark's final comment makes Christina smile. "You know what I really find fascinating? These Florida storms have definite breaks in between. As you reach the end of one you pass through sunshine and then, a little farther on you can see the start of the next downpour. Look, there is the sunshine break coming up now."

Not lifting her head. "Keep looking for those breaks. They are always there between the storms. The sun is always shining behind the clouds - just as in life." He smiles back at her and says, "Mom, that's corny!"

Christina turns her head towards the side window and searches the sky for a glimpse of the rainbow. She discretely lifts her hand to wipe away the remnants of a tear with her sleeve. The clouds part slightly to the east, allowing the sun to reflect the ever-elusive rainbow. She smiles as she sees it and accepts this as her 'heaven-sent' sign. She glances over at Mark saying, "I can see the rainbow."

Mark laughs at her childlike excitement as he replies without moving. "There will be many more rainbows, Mom. You know what? We have fought hard to change the minds and hearts of people along the way in this legal battle. Hopefully, we managed to do that. I have no regrets. But, it would be foolishly egotistical to believe it has not affected us or changed us in almost every way, because it definitely has. We have allowed ourselves to grieve. In fact, we lived through the seven stages of grief. I suppose it is safe to assume that we can't grieve without having loved. Yes, Dad promised me his boats, planes and money, but I was really looking forward to a future with him. At least I now realize that our real life worth is the love we leave behind in the hearts of our loved ones. To me he died a very wealthy man and he left me a valuable inheritance, his love."

The loss of the Rubicon in the "Cape to Rio" yacht race was a shock for all in the Easter Cape area of South Africa. It especially affected the newspaper office where Christina worked as a photojournalist. One of the journalists had been aboard the yacht. It had disappeared without a mayday call or any debris. A gale had hit the competing yachts with many disabled and forced to withdraw from the race. It was believed that the Rubicon was probably swallowed by a rogue wave.

Christina was part of the air search crew. She went out daily in a two propeller plane with the hope of spotting and photographing some yacht debris on the ocean surface. Days of searching followed. Christina's body ached each day from having to lie on the plane floor at the open doorway with camera pointed down at the churning ocean's waves. Although the storm had blown over, there were still the remnants of the Cape winds.

The final day of searching still turned up nothing and they returned to the small airport with great disappointment. They had to return earlier than expected since they had gone out a little further than usual and were running low on fuel.

The small airport landing was going to be difficult since a herd of cattle from a nearby farm had broken through their fence and were on the runway. The pilot swooped over them twice trying to clear the runway. The control tower said they did not expect the plane back so early so they did not have time to clear the cattle. The plane's fuel gauge was on empty. There only alternative was to land on a nearby hill - going up the hill which was an emergency plan that the pilot had executed before. It was a good landing, but meant a long walk back to the airport and a long car ride back to the town of East London. They arrived at their respective homes later than expected.

Dusk was starting to settle over the quaint suburb together with a light rain shower as Christina arrived at the home she shared with her 8 year old son Mark. His concerned little face was pressed against the front window looking for her and then lit up with delight as he spotted her in their driveway. Christina took a photo of her son's "welcome home face" through the window as raindrops fell on the windowpane.

Her newspaper editor liked the photo so much, it made the front page of the next day's edition, marking the end of the stormy weather, as well as the hope and love in a child's eyes.

victims of the martyred...

Chapter TWELVE

Christina and Mark are sitting opposite Sergio at his desk. It is a modestly furnished Miami office with earth-tone decor. The absence of window light is countered by low office overheads and a desk lamp. Sergio is leaning back in his armchair, his arms up and hands clasping the back of his balding head. His expansive posture and large grin reflects his mood.

"You would not have believed it! She actually accused your Uncle Andrew of stealing money out of Richard's office safe at the time of his death. Something like $700,000 in cash! Of course she waited till he left the room before mentioning it. She is not the brightest, you know. Then Gary, your Uncle Andrew's attorney, made the court reporter read back the accusation when Andrew came back into the room. And the joke was that everyone in the room knew Andrew was in Canada when Richard died."

Mark asks, "What did she have to say then?" Now Sergio is laughing aloud. "Oh, then she said that everyone was twisting her words and that she hadn't said that at all. She then said something weird about repeating someone else's words, some partner of your father's."

Christina is laughing now. "Yes, not the brightest!"

Sergio slides some documents across the desk to her and Mark, saying, "Well, I was sure we would receive another settlement offer after the estate curators deposed her. And here we have it. Take a look. I urge you to consider it."

Christina and Mark both push the documents away without glancing at them as Mark says, "You do realize this just shows again how guilty she is. She would not be offering us anything if she weren't. Believe me, she wants it all. The mere fact that she is willing to offer a settlement and some sharing of my father's estate just proves she forged that will and probably was instrumental in his death!"

Sergio lowers his arms and sits forward, elbows on the desk. He looks at them seriously over his spectacles. "I urge you, as your attorney, to reconsider. There will be absolutely nothing left of this estate by the time all the attorneys, and especially your Uncle Andrew, and *his* attorneys, have taken all their fees as estate curators. I've been speaking with Kurt and he feels the same way. From his side, he is also pushing for a settlement."

Christina says flatly, "I'm sure he is. He wants to get paid before the money's gone. Let's get on with her deposition and discuss this afterward. I am pretty sure she'll be offering a completely different scenario after this deposition… I think I heard some noise out front."

Sergio smiles at the familiar sound of Monika's jangling arm bangles before saying, "She knows how to make an entrance!" He motions for Christina and Mark to move into the boardroom through the side door. He tells them he will bring Monika and Kurt through.

As Christina and Mark take their seats they hear the sounds of laughter and congenial conversation. They look at each other with a degree of surprised suspicion. Sergio, Kurt and Monika can be heard through the paper-thin walls. Mark whispers, "You've got to wonder whose attorney he is now, considering he is beginning to taste his money."

Monika, Sergio and Kurt enter the small boardroom smiling. The lack of window light, emphasized by the overhead lighting casts shadows on their faces. The newcomers are all smiling until they notice the stony faces of Christina and Mark. Their mood quickly switches to reflect the professional meeting at hand.

Sergio indicates to Monika to take a seat at the head of the table. Kurt takes up a position to her right and Sergio to the left. Christina and Mark are seated next to each other a couple of chairs away from them and are staring impassively at the three. The deposition begins with Sergio's preliminary questions as to Monika's identity.

Michael and Christina continue to stare impassively at Monika, paying close attention to her answers. For the most part Monika and Kurt are trying very hard to be friendly toward Sergio in the hope of breaking his newfound professional aggressiveness and control. Monika's replies seem carefully rehearsed and are being broken down piece by piece by Sergio's repetitive questioning, with her attorney, Kurt, often forced to intervene to cover up and lead her into her prepared answers.

An hour into the process is beginning to make Monika shift uncomfortably in her seat. She is casually dressed in slacks with T-shirt and has pulled one leg under the other in a display of relaxation. Her arms remain crossed over her chest and the bangles are quiet as she pays close attention to her questioning.

Sergio is leaning into the documents in front of him, glancing up at Monika each time he poses another question to see her reaction. She shifts, straightening her back as he asks the next question.

Suddenly Sergio leans back in his seat holding his documents in his hands. "Now. Tell me again, Mrs. Fischer St. John. Why do you think Richard would have cut his son out of his will?"

Monika's reply is produced along with a sneer on her face. "It is obvious. He was mad at his ex-wife, Christina. She kept trying to get child support out of him. Their child support agreement was signed almost at the same time as this will. It must have been on his mind."

Reacting to Monika's comment, Mark and Christina look at each other in disbelief. Her look of spite is now a characteristic Monika trait. Monika glares spitefully at Christina who looks back at her impassively.

Sergio's next comment is scathing. "How convenient, Mrs. Fischer. You have turned around the evidence we gave you in Mark's deposition to suit your own ends. I believe our claim was that Richard signed this support agreement when he was *supposed* to be signing your will. You're not trying to imply he could be in two places at once? We have proof the agreement was definitely faxed from Pennsylvania where he was at a seminar. He could not have been in Miami signing your will!"

Kurt, on behalf of his client, quickly interjects, "What was that comment meant to mean, Sergio?"

Sergio looks over the top of his glasses at Kurt, then redirects his questions to Monika, "Let's go forward. So you think he was mad at his ex-wife, he did not love his son or, for that matter, his mother, whom he was supporting in a Canadian nursing home. Therefore he cut them all out of his will?"

She looks startled. "No…I don't know. He had not seen Mark for some time after Mark picked a fight with me and my own son."

Sergio grins confidently. "What if I told you he *had* seen his ex-wife and his son? He spoke to them on the phone often until the time of his death. We have telephone records to prove it. In fact, they joined him for lunch a few days before he died. Richard and Mark even made arrangements to meet again the following week."

Monika's eyes widen and her face is etched with angry surprise. Christina looks at her impassively and Mark raises an eyebrow. Kurt shifts uneasily in his seat. Monika's reply is hostile and high-pitched. "I don't believe it. He never saw Mark behind my back, you hear me, never! He would not have done that against my wishes."

Christina glances over at Mark who responds to her with a sarcastic smile. Sergio looks at them and then rolls his eyes at Monika before replying, "Your wishes? So you admit then, you were trying to influence Richard and keep him away from his only son?"

Monika looks down at the table, avoiding everyone's stare. Even Kurt is looking at her with an air of disbelief. She replies in a defensive tone, "That's not what I mean. Everyone knows he was always arguing with Christina. He loved me, not her! He chose to marry me, not his ex-wife!"

Sergio leans forward, elbows on the table, and looks at her, saying, “Okay, then, let me ask you this. Do you think Richard loved his mother and his son?”

She glares back at him and with reluctance, answers, “I suppose so.”

There is a heavy silence as Sergio fingers the pile of documents in front of him. Both Kurt and Monika watch him with apprehension. He pulls out a few pages and slides them across the table to Kurt who looks at them briefly, then places them in front of Monika. Sergio looks at her asking, “Now, do you know where this will came from?”

She does not touch the papers. Her arms are still crossed over her chest. She leans forward and glances at the papers answering, “I am not sure. The first thing I knew shortly after Richard's death is that his office manager, James, disappeared for a while then came back with it, saying, “It’s all okay,” and telling me that I was the one he left everything to.”

Sergio is staring into her eyes intensely as he asks, “What would you say if I told you one of the witnesses whose name is on this will is quite willing to testify that he does not remember signing it in front of you?" She looks wide-eyed and replies, "I don't know what to say."

Kurt looks at her with concern and replies, "Sergio, we have an attorney who claims he prepared this will. Are you saying that he was also lying?"

Sergio grins at Kurt replying, "I can't speak for him and he is not here. Attorneys have been known to lie. I believe you are referring to the attorney Colin Greene who was Richard's in-house attorney? I was told that he moved to Atlanta very suddenly and shortly after Richard's death?"

Sergio looks back at Monika. "Mrs. Fischer St. John, didn't Colin also ask you if he could borrow Richard's Porsche a few days after he died?"

She looks at him with a tightly pulled mouth. Her reply issues through her teeth. "Yes."

Sergio carries on. "You didn't think that was strange?"

Again Monika's responds angrily. "No."

Sergio shakes his head, looks down at the papers for his next question and asks, "What happened to Richard's Bentley?"

Monika answers reluctantly, "Someone took it."

Kurt is startled and looks at her as Sergio continues, “Took it? What if I told you we have a witness who claims you were seen giving it to Samantha, Richard’s illegitimate daughter, to make her go away and not stake a claim against the estate?”

Kurt’s eyes show his concern and he leans forward saying, “I object - hearsay.”

Sergio looks at him with a sarcastic grin and then back at Monika saying, “So, let's go through this again, Mrs. Fischer St. John. You are quite sure Richard was in Florida at the time of signing the will which leaves you sole beneficiary?”

Monika looks relieved the questioning has changed direction and uses her well-rehearsed answer: “Yes, because it was my son's birthday and Richard would not have missed it.”

Sergio continues, “Did you go out for dinner for his birthday? Who was there?”

Once again Monika looks happier with her line of questioning and replies, “Me, my sons, my mother and Richard. He would never have missed my son’s birthday.”

Sergio realizes his questions were expected by Monika. It is obvious that her replies have been well-rehearsed and he goes through them mechanically anyway. “Where did you go for dinner? Do you have any dinner receipts or did Richard pay via credit card?”

Her replies are perhaps a little too quick and sometimes come even before Sergio has finished his question. She continues with repetitive phrases, saying, “I don't know! I can’t recall!”

Sergio stands suddenly and motions for Christina and Mark to follow him out of the room. He looks back at Kurt and Monika, saying, “Excuse us for a few minutes. I am sure you can do with a ten-minute break.” Kurt’s response is a quick, “Yes.”

Christina, Mark and Sergio file out the room and huddle together in the hallway, whispering. Sergio looks from one to the other as he asks, “Are you sure you want me to deliver the final blow? It could either bring a substantially better settlement offer from her if she believes us or it could make her angry enough, if she is not guilty of forgery, to fight back and blow us right out of the water, and then we may have to go to trial.”

Mark whispers back, “Yes. Either way, it works for us. Then we will all know the truth.” Christina adds, “I don't think we have any other option. We have Doreen's affidavit now.

It certainly is an inadvertent helpful indiscretion from Richard. We have already tried to mediate with this witch."

Sergio shrugs his shoulders and takes a deep breath, saying reluctantly, "Okay, then." He gestures for them to follow him back into the boardroom where Kurt and Monika are still seated in silent anticipation. The tension in the room can be cut with a knife as Sergio, Mark and Christina return to their seats.

Sergio clears his throat before launching into his next statement. "Mrs. Fischer St. John, I hope you agree with me that I have been very understanding of your possible grief in your bereavement."

Monika looks at him with a disarming smile. "Yes, you have." Sergio looks down at his papers without focusing on them, but rather to gather the nerve for what is coming next, as he says, "Well, what I have to ask you next is not very easy. Were you aware that your husband was having an affair with his secretary, Doreen, in Toronto? She has given us an affidavit to prove she was with him in a Toronto hotel room the day before his niece's 21st birthday. He took her to the party as well." Sergio stops his line of questioning for a few seconds.

He does not look up from his papers as he continues, "Together with his credit card travel receipts, we can now prove the final stage of his trip, ending with time in Toronto. He was absolutely not here when you claim he signed your will." Everyone turns to catch Monika's reaction.

Monika's arms drop from her chest and the clink of her bangles is the only noise in the utter silence of the room. She goes quite pale. The blood has visibly drained from her face. Her eyelids begin to quiver in the shock of the moment. She looks confused and frightened.

Kurt recoils in shock. He sends a sympathetic look to his client as he launches into a scathing response. "I would hardly call that 'understanding' of my client. This is new to us. Why wasn't this new evidence in the previous discovery you sent? You deliberately kept this from us. We have had not had a chance to investigate this new claim."

Sergio, obviously annoyed with this accusation, looks up at him and in a low tone answers, "Because we only received the affidavit from Doreen yesterday. Kurt, I can only give you this information as fast as I am able to receive it. So, here it is!"

Monika is looking at her hands and rubbing the palms together. Her face is still pale and her glazed eyes stare at the table top. She mutters, “I don't believe it! I don’t believe it!”

Christina is taking it all in. For the first time, she sees something representing emotion or grief on Monika’s face. Only it is grief for herself, not for her dead husband.

Sergio looks at Monika with some sympathy in his eyes. “I am sorry, Mrs. Fischer. I know this must be painful but it is true, and now we are waiting for the hotel credit card receipts to prove the timing.”

Kurt is angry. He pushes his chair back forcefully and stands. “Sergio, this deposition is over! We are leaving! Or do you have any further surprises for my client?”

Sergio looks up at him calmly. “No, Kurt, that’s it, for now… but we reserve the right to depose your client again once we have the new evidence in hand. Let me walk you out.” He turns to look at Christina and Mark who are watching Monika not with the expected reaction of self-satisfied revenge, but rather as confidant accusers. Monika’s head is downcast and her shoulders rounded as she walks out the room.

Kurt says a brief and courteous parting goodbye to Christina and Mark as he follows Sergio out. Sergio closes the door behind them.

Mark and Christina sit quietly and look at each other, their relief evident. They are listening to the audible voices on the other side of the door.

Sergio is apologizing to Kurt and Monika for his line of questioning and for delivering the final, brutal blow. Mark overhears both attorneys commenting on the fact that Richard was obviously a jerk of a husband. Although its intention is possibly to alleviate Monika's embarrassment, Mark is annoyed at the remark about his father. He looks at his mother with a raised eyebrow and whispers, "I really don't like the friendliness going on between those two guys. It is clear who the jerks are, and it does not include Dad."

Christina whispers back. "I am not surprised. They can taste the money. Remember what the judge was overheard saying after the last hearing for the increase in attorney's fees? This case has been a feeding frenzy for attorneys' legal fees."

The kill was fairly humane. The Impala (deer) was brought down by a pride of lions at the waterhole. It was fast as two lionesses acted as executioners. Both suffocated the buck with their powerful jaws locked onto either side of its throat. This was the first time Christina had witnessed an animal kill first-hand. She was fifteen years old and on a school trip to the Kruger National Park in South Africa. She would never forget the turmoil of emotions she felt at that moment in time. The obvious need for nature to replenish and feed - opposed to the violence of an innocent's death. The rifle-wielding game ranger with them had spotted the "kill" scene play out and stopped the Land Rover for the group to bear witness. With a South African accented voice, he told the students this was something mostly seen on film and they would now have a very unique experience. Christina had almost wished he hadn't stopped the vehicle. This scene would be embedded in her soul forever.

As part of the educational experience, the game ranger then explained the order of the feed. "The lions and lionesses will eat first, then their cubs fight over the meat that might be left. This is the natural order of things and it becomes about the survival of the fittest. Then the vultures scavenge whatever is left over and do nature's clean up. If another scavenger - like a hyena gets into the mix, the lions and the vultures would all be scared off. This time, the Impala probably did not know what hit it. There is a body chemistry that happens to the victim at the time of the kill. It goes into a quiet, subdued shock.

The pride has a careful strategy planned when it lies in wait at the watering hole. Normally it's the lionesses that give chase after a herd of Impala or zebra or other wildlife, attacking the stragglers which could be the oldest, sickest or youngest."

hearts grown cold...

Chapter THIRTEEN

It is not quite dusk as Christina walks along the quiet corridor of the North Palm Beach School. Her high heels echo on the cement. She is glancing at the numbers on royal blue classroom doors as she passes them, now and then peering through a window framed by blue and white walls. She has not told Mark about this school meeting, but instead suggested he should share a pizza at home with his friends, happy to see him doing something ordinary with his peers for a change.

The final showdown with Monika and her lawyer is still playing itself out in her head, even as she readies herself for the possible ordeal ahead. She had a call from the Mark's school counselor, the one who deals with the students' college applications. He has asked her to come in "for a talk," and she has no idea what it might be about, but she fears the worst. The last few weeks of depositions, charges and countercharges have taken its toll on Mark. With all the pressures of his senior year and getting into a good school, he might have snapped. He may have broken a rule, or someone's head, for that matter, although she knows her son is not violent by nature. Could it be slipping grades, again?

She finds the right door number and knocks. The door opens quickly and she is greeted with a warm handshake. She looks somewhat relieved. The counselor looks at her over his dark-rimmed glasses as he ushers her to the wooden chair in front of his file-covered desk. She takes her seat, crosses her legs and adjusts her pink skirt to cover her knees. She leans back crossing her arms over a crisp white shirt. The middle-aged man is dressed in a conservative brown suit and his face is expressionless as he sits down behind the desk. He frowns and taps his pen on a sheaf of papers. He launches right into the conversation. "This is Mark's college-entry essay, Mrs. St. John. I would like you to read it."

She looks mystified. "Is there a problem? Is it an acceptable essay?"

"Oh, it's acceptable alright. I really need to know how much of it is factual or merely his amazing creative imagination. This is supposed to be a personal essay, one that shows what kind of person the student is, what his outlook on life is, what his hopes and dreams are."

Christina asks the obvious. "And Mark's essay?"

"Well, it may be one of the best I have ever read, but it really seems to be unbelievable. Take a look at it." The man pushes the paper to her side of the table.

Christina uncrosses her arms, picks it up and reads the title aloud: "Life on the Conservation Game Farm." She smiles, anticipating the story. She begins to read silently with tears welling in her eyes: *Winter in South Africa is best described as dry and extremely cold. Every winter I went to spend two weeks with my grandmother in a small town called East London. My grandmother managed the restaurant and worked on a wild life nature preserve called Mpongo Park, about twenty miles out of town. Then I spent one winter with her that changed my life and my view of wild animals.*

It was a cold morning in December. I woke up around 7:00 and got ready for the day. While I was getting dressed, I could feel the freezing air on my skin, and my grandmother suggested adding my leather jacket as an outer layer. This was one of the coldest days ever recorded, so before leaving the house I put on about four layers of clothing. I did not know at the time just how advantageous this would be later that day.

The wind hit my face and I felt the chill run through every vein and artery in my body. We proceeded to walk up a hill to my grandmother's restaurant. As we were walking we could hear all the animals sending out their morning cries, but the most predominant were the lions' roars. The day went like any other and I helped everywhere I could. I served customers and sometimes even helped in the kitchen. However, whenever I could I would stop to observe the hippopotamuses fighting in the water for male dominance. The restaurant was warm and the outside cold seemed like a far-off place. One thing that really annoyed me, however, was that the African gray parrot that my grandmother owned would not stop squawking at me all day.

At the end of the day, my mother came up from the house with Sheba, my grandmother's lion cub, and Cindy, a young lady who helped my grandmother raise other lion cubs. I fed the cub and got my mother some hot chocolate to help her deal with the icy temperatures. Cindy helped my grandmother prepare an early dinner for all of us. Cindy then suggested that my mother should get her camera, and go visit a lion that she had raised two years ago. His name was Jabulani, a two-year-old male lion that had been raised with about ten baboons and ate bananas before he ate red meat.

We left the restaurant when the sun was not far from setting. We all walked up the cold gravel drive as the cold winter air pierced my wool gloves and sent shivers up my spine. We stood in front of the enclosure where the lion lay in the corner on the cement floor with a baboon sleeping on his back. My mother had taken a few pictures when Cindy suggested getting some pictures of me hugging the lion, assuring us that he was tame. She proceeded to lead us into the cage. She entered first, my mother and I followed. Everything appeared to be calm, until I entered. Within seconds, the baboons were flying through the air letting out piercing screeches. One jumped from the fence and landed on my shoulder and its teeth went through my clothing as though I wore nothing, scraping my shoulder muscle. The pain was incredible; however, my instant reflex had me punching the baboon until it released. My mother and Cindy were catching baboons flying through the air at me. My mother took control and immediately turned me around to start pulling me out.

All I could do was stare at her face when it turned white with horror as I felt a huge pair of arms engulf my waist. The lion, weighing about four hundred pounds, had come up behind me and instinctively was trying to rip me to the ground in order to tear my throat out. My mother's grip tightened and she stared into the eyes of Jabulani as his claws tore straight through my clothing. I could feel them touch the skin of my abdomen. The only words my mother spoke were, "You cannot have my son!" and the lion's response was a defiant roar. My mind was racing and I thought of everything I had done and still wanted to do in my life. At that point, I thought my life was over. My mother's strength was amazing in the tug of war. Her pulling caused the claws around my stomach to begin to tear into my leather jacket. Cindy ran over and hit Jabulani on the nose. Instantly he released his grip and one single claw came up and cut my right cheek. My mother pulled me out as Cindy closed the gate. Jabulani glared at us over his shoulder as he paced up and down the wired fence. I spent the rest of the day in a state of shock. All

I could think of was what had just happened to me. My grandmother (who thankfully was an experienced Red Cross nurse) helped patch my bloody cheek and I spent a restless night.

The next morning I returned to see Jabulani. His sleek, muscular body was spread out across the floor. He had just been fed half a dead cow; the hair around his mouth was still covered in blood. He raised his head and his eyes fixed onto mine. It felt as though he was peering into my soul. He did nothing, as though he had no remorse, no shame, no fear: all he did was stare at me. It was at this moment I realized that the wild instincts could no longer be suppressed from being brought up by humans. He was a lion and amazingly his actions were to protect a fellow animal. I found a new respect that day for all living creatures. No matter what, the wild instincts in a naturally wild animal will always come out at some point. The current scar on my cheek remains a token of the vivid memory.

Cindy, basically the only mother Jabulani had ever known, felt that it was time to let him return to the wild since he had become a true lion and she could no longer treat him as anything else. She also felt his sudden attack on me could have been due to my child's size being recognized by Jabulani as the same as that of the tourist children who had been teasing and throwing things at him recently through the surrounding fence. I have always thanked my mother for not giving up on me. She gave me a wonderful example of how to always hold onto what I love, even if I have to risk my own life.

as a story is told...

Chapter FOURTEEN

The warm wood-paneled room is rustically elegant. Large black-and-white cowhide-covered armchairs framed by bull horns are artistically placed around a large rug. To the side of a solid wooden desk there is a fun antique cowboy-shaped slot machine.

The large room reflects the rich history of a Kissimmee, Florida cattle-farming family. There are numerous rodeo photos, emblems and riding trophies along a wall. Family photos cover another entire wall - a long history of faces topped off by Stetson hats, creatively framed, proudly displayed.

One wall is carved with the life-size shapes of three men on horseback and it overshadows the room. A large Stetson hat is on the corner of the desk chair and a Florida Gator's flag hangs off the front of the desk.

The faint noises of an awakening farm can be heard through an open window. The smells of the cattle farm mixed with the aroma of brewing morning coffee waft through the warm air of the house. Christina enters the room carrying a mug of coffee. She is dressed in jeans and blouse. Her long hair is still a little damp from her morning shower. Behind her is a small-framed woman whose body resembles that of a teenager, but the weathered face of wisdom and gray hair exposes the truth of a woman in her sixties. She is dressed in a long, white T-shirt and shorts. Anne Carter is holding her cup with both hands.

Christina sits in one of the armchairs and Anne takes the other as she says, “I am sorry you have to leave so early, my friend. I was hoping we could visit for a few more days. We had a lot of fun over dinner last night. You know you are always welcome. I enjoy having you here.”

Christina smiles warmly. “Thank you, Anne. I value your friendship. Being here in your welcoming home and having this time together restores my sanity in a very insane world.”

Anne pulls one leg under the other, displaying a shapely calf muscle. She looks at Christina through thick lenses. “I know, my friend. It has been a nightmare for you and Mark. Richard must be turning in his grave watching this. Everything he worked so hard for is being eaten away by the attorneys.”

Christina is sipping her coffee slowly. "I know. My privilege was sharing in his rags-to-riches life. Pity the riches went to his head. That's when he made some poor choices."

Anne replies, "Choices that lead to his death. I told you before I took an instant dislike to Monika. She was crude and totally disrespectful, trying to impress Richard and his friends with sexual jokes. Then for God's sake, she was dressed in tight gym shorts in a prestigious Palm Beach hotel!"

Anne gets up, placing her mug on the table, and walks across to the bookshelves. She continues, reaching for a coffee table book. "I still have a book Richard gave us after you arrived and we all went on the horse trail together. Here it is. The words he wrote in the front still baffle me. *From my family to yours, signed Richard, Christina and Mark.*"

She leans over Christina's shoulder and points to the writing at the front of the book before saying, "Then two weeks later he has shacked up with the stepmother from hell! Poor Mark. I could see how excited he was to be back with his dad."

Christina's face reflects the painful memory. "Yes, she worked fast and hard. She managed to manipulate Richard purely on a sexual and flattery level, all this while we were packing up in Africa. She understood his phobias and needs well. Thank God he woke up to the fact toward the end and reconnected with Mark. Mark was so looking forward to their next lunch together. Still think it is incredible that he had to sneak away to see his own son."

Anne sits down again holding the book on her lap as she says, "You know that he was separating from her and he was sick of her kids? This was only a few weeks before he died." She laughs as she says, "I can still see him standing in front of that window fixing his hair in the reflection. He thought I was not watching. He was a very charming and good-looking man."

Christina looks at the window almost expecting to see his reflection and then sadly looks back at Anne. "God, I hope that phone call I made to Monika wasn't the death knell for him. Remember that voice mail I told you about? In his phone call to me, he said he would walk right out the door if he thought she was there only for his money and if she was trying to cut out Mark. He actually told me that his estate was being left to Mark and his mother.

I realized later that she had finally heard who was to inherit his estate and from his own mouth! I told him she was always making up stories about Mark each time he visited, trying to hurt their relationship. She was standing right next to him during the call. I could hear her ranting, but it suddenly stopped when he said that Mark was to inherit his estate. Actually, I think he may even have said that for her to hear."

Anne looks at her with sorrowful eyes. "He was not a stupid man but he was definitely a manipulated man. I still remember the Christmas before Richard died, when Mark asked his father if he could see him. She had the audacity to say that he had to have lunch with her and Richard first. Then she would decide if he could spend time with them again."

Anne pauses, trying to compose her rising anger. She takes a slow sip of her coffee before continuing, "Poor kid, he swallowed a lot to maintain the bond with his father. Of course, Richard knew he was hurting you by hurting your son. He never forgave you for leaving him." Christina grimaces, "I often ask myself if I should have just stayed and turned a blind eye to the womanizing - like she did. Surely she must have known."

Anne shakes her head and says, "I would never have been able to. I don't think she knew he was still having affairs. He found the perfect, narcissistically stupid wife. Her ego was larger than this farm." They both laugh at that and the mood lightens.

Anne pauses for a moment as she reflects on their great bond. Her eyes reflect her warm thoughts as she continues, "I am so pleased y'all got together that week before he died and Mark heard from his father that he was proud of him. At least he has that. Richard called me and said he had really enjoyed seeing you both. I could not help but tease him a little by saying he chose the wrong Mrs. St. John this time. Oh, yes, didn't she want you to stop calling yourself Mrs. St John?"

Christina responds to Anne's comment with a smirk and says "Such a stupid little girl from the wrong side of the tracks." Anne continues, "That was funny. Obviously she always knew you were a threat to her financial prospects. They did kill him; you do realize that, don't you?"

Christina looks at her and says softly, "I know, and we would never have known the truth if you had not given me that newspaper report at the funeral. Thanks again, Anne, we would have still believed the heart attack story and not the truth about the jet-ski collision. We have so much to be grateful to you for. I still can't believe I did not know what Home Shopping was when we arrived from Africa. Then, you just happened to know the owner. If you had not made the introduction I would never have gotten on my feet and been able to stay in the States. "

Anne grins as she says, "You took it from there. You made it work and Richard was really proud of you. I still remember seeing you on TV and calling him. You were doing so well and I wanted to tell him. Of course, his reply was, 'Yes, I taught her everything she knows!' Then we both laughed so hard. He was not happy about your success in the beginning. In fact, he was mad that you became independent again and he lost the control, but he was still proud of you."

Christina throws her head back laughing, "Richard even admitted to it at that last lunch. He said I'd been right, he was a control freak. I thought his honesty was because he was getting older, but you have to wonder if his soul knew his inevitable destiny." Anne nods in agreement adding, "God works in mysterious ways. Richard was surrounded by many non-believers. He never knew how to distinguish between friends. Sometimes, he chose them merely because they propped up his self-esteem. There is a fine line between goodness and evil."

Christina looks at her thoughtfully. "Funny, Richard used to say there was a fine line between love and hate - as well as ethics in business. A line he believed he could cross and come away unscathed. Mark used to say that we loved to hate each other, because we hated to love each other."

Anne looks at her and with a sigh says, "Wise young man. Well, Monika did not get away with crossing that fine line. Yep, there is a fine line between godliness and lawlessness. She may think she got away with what she did, but there is a Divine justice on the other side waiting for her. God will not forgive her for the hurt she has caused you, your son, and Richard. Anyway, I am really pleased Mark managed to start college and was even accepted into three. I know his dad was looking forward to that news. How is he doing? Is the case finally settled? "

Christina sighs deeply and holds her mug with both hands. “Well, very well. His college grades are good and he still talks about wanting to be a doctor. So, we will see.”

Christina shifts in her seat as she uncrosses a leg to cross the other. “We at last agreed to this final settlement. It is difficult to understand why we had to settle with the person who probably killed Richard just to stop the attorneys from taking everything. Another difficulty has been the fact that Mark's uncle Andrew just does not get it. At this late date, he has filed for even more money from the estate for his own fees, especially now that we have settled the case. Really, Anne, there is hardly anything left. The final sum we may get will just go to my accumulated debts and lawyers’ fees. That’s another aspect that has really hurt Mark. Richard’s side of the family was all he had left of his father. Now those relationships are damaged, too.”

Anne has a rueful smile as she stands and walks toward the window. She looks out at her farm pensively. “We miss Richard. I pray for his peace every day. He must be so regretful now, looking at all of this.”

Christina looks at her with gratitude. “Thank you. I know it was tough to stay friends with both of us. Richard really valued your opinions and friendship.”

Christina stands and stretches out for Anne’s mug on the table saying, “I can get you another coffee. Did I tell you that Monika had the audacity to offer Mark his father’s wave-runner after the final settlement? Of course this was a verbal offer, via her attorney, and not in writing.”

They walk towards the kitchen together. Anne looks angry as she continues. “She is totally lacking in feeling! You mean the only possible evidence at the murder scene? The same wave-runners that she said were lost on the side of the highway immediately after the so-called accident that killed Richard?”

Christina sighs and says, “Yes, the same ones. They were hidden with a private eye she hired at his Palm Beach Gardens home. You never know, it could be the same person who did her the favor of cutting my brake lines. It was eerie to know he lived that close to us.”

Anne leans back on the wooden kitchen counter and looks at her with wide eyes behind thick glasses. “Now that the police have the wave-runners, surely they can do something?”

Christina says, “No. Too little, too late. The police are not even willing to take my calls now. They still think this is all a family battle over money and a civil suit thing. Mark told her to stick the wave-runners. She just could not help making that final jab to his heart.”

Anne has her arm around Christina’s waist as they leave the warmth of the farm kitchen, coffee mugs in-hand. Anne’s voice is tinged with resentment as she replies, “She is a cold. I wish her God’s entire wrath. This is what she deserves.”

A young cowboy bursts through the front door just as the two women settle in their living room chairs. He is sandy-haired, radiating energy and dressed in cowboy gear. His boots are noisy on the wooden floor. He grins, takes off his hat as he enters and says, “Morning, Mama. Morning, Christina. Is Dad here?”

Anne replies, “Nope, he is with the hands at the lake. There are a couple of cows in the mud.” He turns just as quickly and heads out the door with a quick, “Bye.”

Christina laughs. "Your family is just the way we always imagined the American ranching family to be, with all the good standards and the very best human qualities."

Anne grins proudly. "Thank you for that. We are all here for you and consider you as one of our very best friends."

Christina smiles her thanks. She swallows the last of her coffee as she gets ready to leave. Christina bends to pick up her bag at the doorway while Anne sighs deeply and opens the front door. The bright morning sunlight illuminates Anne's pale skin and small red marks on her face. She pulls her long T-shirt down a little over her shorts and well-shaped legs.

Christina looks at Anne and her good-humored comment makes them both laugh. "Please God; I have legs as good as yours one day!"

Anne responds with, "Please God I am as tall and brave as you are one day! The school gymnastics helped my legs, but the Florida sun has really not been kind to my pale skin. I have another round of chemo this week for the skin cancer on my face. All part of my farm life I suppose. You hurry back when you can. Give my love to Mark and be strong, both of you. Watch your back, my friend."

Anne hugs Christina tightly before the latter steps down from the white wooden porch covered in spiky moss. Christina turns to wave a final goodbye as she wipes a warm tear from under her sunglasses. She gets into her SUV parked in the dirt. Anne is still waving and standing on her porch long after the SUV leaves the farm, churning the dust of the dirt road behind it.

Christina looks back at Anne in her rear view mirror. She smiles at the fact that Anne is lingering on the porch and opens her window to give a last wave as some of the red dust enters the vehicle. She coughs and quickly closes her window.

The red African dust is swirling into sporadic mini tornadoes around a young Christina. She looks down at her little bare feet dusted red with bits of dry grass between her toes. Her blue and white polka dot skirt is flaring with the sudden wind gusts. She holds the side of her hair down and away from her squinting, blue eyes. Looking up at the sky she realizes storm clouds are rolling in fast.

Leaving her stick drawings in the sand, she turns and skips towards the thatched cottage. She quickly chases some of the little chicks pecking in the dirt into their covered area. Her action alerts the geese near the cottage doorway who then chase her running through the front door - which then remains open behind her. The geese are standing guard.

She calls out to her sister. "Jenny there is a storm coming. So we will have rainwater for a bath tonight. This time I don't have to share your bath water. Yay! I also got the baby chicks in. But I wish the geese would leave me alone. They are always chasing me back into the house!"

Laughter is heard from an older, teasing woman's voice inside the cottage. "They are guarding the house - and us. In any case, they only chase naughty little girls. Stay inside now. Mom and Dad are running late from town...."

Suddenly there is a loud bang in the cottage interrupting Jenny's voice. Seconds before, Christina had gone through the kitchen doorway. She turns to see a large streaking flash of blue light pass behind her down the passage.

Jenny appears from the living room dressed in her 60's look - a pretty brunette with big hair, slender slacks and mid-drift top. Looking at Christina, she asks, "What on earth was that?"

Christina looks confused. She is pointing. "There was a big blue light that went that way."

Jenny looks in the direction of Christina's finger. "My God!" That was lightning and it hit the phone. It is all melted. Look at the black burn marks on the wall. You have angels taking care of you Christina - that could have been you!"

Christina asks with a sincere and quizzical look, "Then I am not so naughty. I have angels and maybe the geese are angels too?"

the power of love…

Chapter FIFTEEN

Christina is seated in a hospital vinyl green armchair, one elbow resting on the wooden arm handle. Her chin is resting in the cup of her hand. She stares "trance-like" at the rise and fall of her son, Mark's chest, covered in a white sheet. The large plastic tube taped into his mouth quivers as each breath of air is forced into his lungs. She glances occasionally at the other tubes from various parts of Mark's body leading to blinking lights, graphs and noisy monitors. Mark's 6 ft. 5 inch frame barely fits the ICU hospital bed. He is in an induced coma.

Christina sighs deeply and turns her head towards the "poker-faced" uniformed nurse entering the room (ICU ward) wheeling a machine towards Mark. She stands up with a stretch of her back and greets the nurse in welcome relief. "Hi Nurse Joan. I am pleased you are here. I really need that bathroom break!" The nurse looks concerned and says. "Off you go! You have hardly moved from this room in the last two days. In fact you only leave when you have to go to the restroom!"

Christina is gone in flash down the stark white hallway and she is back in the room just as quickly.

The nurse greets Christina's return with a knowing smile, followed with a caring question. "Do you need anything? Perhaps a magazine to read? Do have any other family that can come and be with you at this time?"

Christina does not respond to the questions immediately. Instead, she takes a deep breath through her teeth and in a quiet voice asks, "Are his vitals still holding steady?"

The nurse replies in similar whispered tones. "All the same, no change. He is a very strong young man. It is a miracle he is still with us. However the doctor is not willing to move him to JFK unless we can stabilize him more"

Christina follows this with, "Yes, he is a very strong and courageous young man. I am so proud of him. He is still holding on. I just wish the attending doctor had transported Mark to JFK when we first arrived in the ER two days ago - when he was still stable, before his heart attack yesterday. I understand the urgency, but still can't believe that they decided to cut open his chest in a hospital without a cardiac unit! The cardiac doctor who was called in even admitted to this all common mistake. He also admitted to putting the first stint directly into Mark's heart and not into the fluid around it! I have been asking Mark to be strong...I know he can hear me when I am next to him, even in his coma. Yes, my brother is on a plane from the UK and he should be here by tomorrow."

The nurse moves closer to Christina saying. "Mark can definitely hear you. We are always careful what we say near him. I know from experience that coma patients can hear every word in the room. Some have even come around and told us what we said around them, word-for-word!"

Christina pauses shaking her head side to side, "I am sorry, I should not be venting at you. All of the nurses in the ICU have been terrific. Thank you and thanks for the magazine offer. I have truly been 'zoning out' and re-living random memories. Mark has gone through so much in his lifetime. He lost his father, went through an awful estate battle and had to sacrifice his final college year to get through the legal battle. He still maintains his great character of care and kindness to all, when others may have become psycho killers. He became my protector, best friend and business partner. He is really great at all he does!"

The nurse is inquisitive as she asks. "What business are the two of you in?"

Christina's response is one of playful pride. "Marketing and business development. But, Mark is truly the innovator and visualizer. He makes projects happen effortlessly and helps me look really good! We were working hard on finishing books to highlight all those that *make a difference* in their communities. Strangely enough, when we came into the ER, Mark made me promise that I would finish these books. I told him that he was not going anywhere. We have too much to still do! I am so grateful that God gave me this wonderful baby boy. He is one of the few young men in this world who was mature enough and confident enough to be proud of being close to his mother. This is especially difficult in a world of profiling and bias!"

The nurse smiles, nods knowingly and says, "He is still protecting you. He will wait for your brother. He does not want you to be alone..." Then she stops abruptly realizing what she just was about to say.

Christina realizes the same. She stands up, walking across the shiny white vinyl floor to Mark's bedside. She reaches over the bed's side railing and strokes his forehead reassuringly. Christina continues her conversation.

"I know your shift started today and you weren't part of the first two days. Do you know that after his heart attack the doctor said my son would probably not recognize me? That he was not expected to get through that night? Now you know that he must have heard all of that too. Well, here we are. Look at how strong he is. Well, he did recognize his mother. When I was allowed back into the room he was in a lifeless state. But, he managed to smile at the corners of his mouth to show me he knew I was there. Then he took it a step further and there was an incredible golden glow that shone through his face at me. I am sure I saw his spirit at that moment. He followed this by making his blood pressure go crazy and that same doctor came running back in saying that Mark obviously did know I was here! "

The nurse laughs and grins widely through her reply, "Yes, truly a miracle. Nurse Emily, who was on duty at the time told me. Everyone was quite shocked considering he was gone for almost eight minutes."

Still stroking Mark's forehead, Christina turns towards the sound of rain hitting the window. She looks down at him with a smile, "Hey, remember the day we talked about the sun will shine just as quickly? It's always shining behind those storm clouds. I know you said I was being corny. Well, here we are again fighting another life battle. I really need you to fight hard this time Mark... you know your mommy needs you. Many need you!"

Tears are welling in Christina's eyes and sobs tearing at her throat. She quickly regains her stoic composure to protect her son's feelings. She looks at the window and then at the nurse, who is preparing to leave the room. Christina's comment is aimed at the nurse's retreating back.

"I really wish I could open a window. I still can't get used to the fact we now have an air-conditioned existence and the windows are always sealed. I miss the smell of the wet earth and clean crisp air after the rain. I know Mark does as well."

The nurse turns her head and replies. "Yes, me too. My life is almost completely air-conditioned."

Christina nods her a goodbye and looks towards the doorway. She feels secure in the fact that the new nursing shift has arrived. The male night nurse is now seated just outside the door punching Mark’s recent body vitals into the computer. Christina has grown accustomed to the ICU system and a genuine bond has developed between her and the nurses.

Christina remains at Mark's bedside. She gazes pensively at the window. A red-dusk sunset is starting to shine through the pelting rain. Her eyes glaze over as her mind drifts back into their world of memories. Lost in these thoughts, a smile plays with the corners of her mouth as she whispers encouragement and reminders to her son.

"Another storm ends Mark. There is a beautiful sunset outside. Really wish you could see it. You said that these Florida thunderstorms are so much like those we had in Africa - the type of storms that arrive suddenly and can be torrential, but then are over just as quickly. You have so many people who love you and are praying for you. I don't want you to worry about Chanel. I have Mary looking after the house and keeping an eye on the dogs. Mary says Chanel is waiting patiently for you at the front door."

Quite suddenly, Mark's eyes open wide as though in shock. He quite literally re-enters his body as the night nurse enters the room relaying a telephone message. "Mark's aunt from South Africa called. She was asking how he is doing and sends her love to you both."

After seeing Mark's open eyes, the night nurse turns sharply on his heels to call the attending doctor, as well as the floor nurse. The white-uniformed medical team rushes in. They are very surprised that Mark's eyes are open and that he is clearly registering thoughts. His eyes are darting around the room in search of something familiar. They then come to rest on his mother's face.

At first glance, the doctor looks somewhat skeptical. He looks at the hovering nurses saying that this could merely be a reflex. Christina pulls up the corner of her mouth at him in a sneering reply. The night nurse takes his pen-like flash light from his pocket, moving it across the front of Mark's eyes. The doctor's demeanor changes when he sees Mark's reaction. He is obviously surprised at the fact that Mark's pupils are moving with the direction of the light. The nurses smile at Mark and acknowledge his presence.

Christina giggles with delight. Then understanding that Mark has the ventilator tube in his mouth, she asks. "Mark blink twice for yes and once for no. Can you see us? Are you back?" Mark blinks twice and for the next few minutes maintains the blinking conversation process. The nurses bear witness to an incredible moment in time.

"Have you been listening to all that has been said around you?" Mark blinks his yes.

Christina's forehead furrows as she asks." Are you in pain?" Mark blinks once and the relief on her face is evident.

Mark blinks twice again when Christina says, "I really love you Mark and hope you can stay. Please keep fighting. But if heaven is calling - I will be there with you one day. In the meantime please send me signs so I know you are okay. I am your forever mother and will always be worrying about you." Then almost immediately after her last word, Mark closes his eyes returning to his deep sleep state. There is a positive energy shift in the room. The nurses look at Christina with broad smiles of renewed hope. Only then does she notice the doctor had left at some point during her eye conversation with Mark. The nurses continue their work of checking monitors and the night nurse pulls the curtain around Mark to do his nightly wash.

Christina goes back to her family vigil role in the green armchair behind the curtain. There is an element of relaxed hope in her face as she returns to her thoughts.

Once the curtain is pulled back to expose her son's bed, Christina curls into her fetal position in the armchair. The nurse hands a blanket to Christina's outstretched hand. She pulls it roughly over her jean-clad legs and watches the nurse pull Mark's blanket up to his neck. He also makes sure Mark's feet are covered. Christina thanks him with a peaceful smile.

The rain on the windowpane begins to slow to a light drizzle, allowing Christina to hear the distant familiar voice of a newscaster reporting on the local weather coming from the TV in the staff break room.

"Well, this is the price we pay for living in paradise - the occasional thunderstorm. There is another one on the radar coming in from the east, but it promises to be a short one. For all the avid boaters out there, be careful on the water tomorrow morning. Swells will be at about eight feet with wind gusts of 30 knots. Later in the day, we have clear skies and sunshine all day, unlike our friends to the north who are experiencing snow flurries. In fact, we have a week full of sunshine and only some scattered thunderstorms. Now, we have something special to show you. It was sent in from one our viewers earlier today. Yes, there it is – a beautiful photo of a large rainbow seen over the ocean after the first storm worked through the coastal areas. Gorgeous scene isn't it? Framed by the sunshine after that thunderstorm? You know what? It almost looks heaven-sent!"

Mark died peacefully the next afternoon with his mother at his side – shortly after the arrival of his uncle.

Warriors of Change

A bitter struggle fought...
to change human thought.

A welcome death...
for a broken soul.

New freedom...
from an earthly goal.

Warm tears shed...
for the departed.

Angry warriors...
victims of those martyred.

Hearts grown cold...
as a story is told.

The power of love...
Burns in truth above!

50246854R00182

Made in the USA
Charleston, SC
19 December 2015